Malignant Humors

Malignant Humors

Selected Stories
Crad Kilodney

Black Moss Press

Published by Black Moss Press with the assistance of
the Canada Council and the Ontario Arts Council.

Black Moss Press books are distributed by Firefly Books Ltd.,
3520 Pharmacy Ave., Unit 1-C, Scarborough, Ontario, M1W 2T8

CANADIAN CATALOGUING IN PUBLICATION DATA
Kilodney, Crad
Malignant humors
ISBN 0-88753-170-9
I. Title.
PS8571.I46M34 1988   C813'.54   C88-093745-9
PR9199.3.K55M34 1988

ACKNOWLEDGEMENTS
The stories in this collection appeared previously in the following
Canadian, American or British publications:
*Descant, Carolina Qtly., DaVinci, Grinning Idiot, Nicotine Soup,
Chock, Not Guilty, Only Paper Today, Junction,* and *What.*
They also appeared in these earlier books by the author:
*Mental Cases, World Under Anaesthesia, Gainfully Employed In
Limbo, Lightning Struck My Dick, Human Secrets – Book Two,
The Green Book, The Scarlet Book* and *The Orange Book.*

Correspondence with the author may be directed to
Crad Kilodney, Charnel House,
P.O. Box 281, Station 'S',
Toronto, Ontario, M5M 4L7.

Cover photograph by Tim McKenna.
Hand-tinted by Phil McLeod.

Contents

Introduction

Actually, there is no introduction. I did write one but when I showed it to a distinguished colleague of mine, she was so horrified she urged me not to print it or I would cause a great deal of trouble, offend a lot of people and possibly destroy my career. I considered the matter as calmly and rationally as I could and had to agree that it was indeed so unspeakably horrible as to be unprecedented in the history of literature. I was in a bad mood when I wrote it, but that's no excuse.

It's really too bad because there were some terrific lines in it, and a lot of the inside information I revealed about certain publishers was extremely funny.

But you don't have to take my word for it. No, indeed. YOU CAN RECEIVE AN UNCENSORED, UNEXPURGATED COPY OF THE ORIGINAL INTRODUCTION TO THIS BOOK THAT HAD TO BE SUPPRESSED BECAUSE OF ITS HORRIBLE NATURE! Just send a self-addressed stamped envelope and ONE DOLLAR to me at my private mailing address as listed elsewhere in this book. The number of copies of this rare, collectible document will be STRICTLY LIMITED TO THE NUMBER OF REQUESTS RECEIVED, SO ACT NOW!

C.K.

Lightning Struck My Dick

I am lying on the beach thinking about Leon Czolgosz.

Leon Czolgosz goes to a factory to look for a job. The foreman does not like his looks. 'Sorry, chum,' he says. 'No jobs today. Nyah ha ha!'

Leon is in the park feeding crumbs to ducks in the pond. One bites him on the finger.

A movie is playing in a tiny theater in a small college town – *The Leon Czolgosz Story*. No one is watching it.

Leon Czolgosz is in grammar school. The teacher has a hard time pronouncing his name. The other children laugh at him. He runs away.

Much depressed, Leon visits a brothel for some romantic diversion. He is introduced to a shy, young girl of studious temperament. Minutes later, joined in passionate embrace, he is about to reach his peak when she comments, 'I don't much care for Bulwer-Lytton. Do you?'

Leon is in the public library to return a book. It is overdue and he refuses to pay the fine. 'My taxes pay for these books!' he snarls at the librarian. She hits him over the head with Locke's *Treatise on Civil Government*.

Leon goes into a novelty shop and buys a harmonica. He sits in the back of a bus playing a Chopin Polonaise. A fat lady of German descent knocks the instrument out of his mouth with an umbrella and steps on it. Leon is too chivalrous to strike a lady. Instead, he vows, 'I will murder someone and they will name a mountain after me.'

Ah, there are nice black clouds on the horizon. A storm is coming up. Some of the people are beginning to leave. But I do not leave. Neither do the crabs. Where are the crabs anyway? Are they hiding?

I would like to speak to a crab, to ascertain first-hand the Platonic form of crab-ness. I can imagine a crab crawling along the sand beside me. I say, 'Hello, crab.' The crab does not answer. Is the crab reading my thoughts?

In the movie *The Attack of the Crab Monsters,* the giant crabs speak by telepathy and intimidate some people on a tiny island. Each night they chop off a piece of the island and force people into a smaller area. Finally the people kill them with positive electricity. Such is the virtue of Norman Vincent Peale's book.

I am walking through a deserted alley, anticipating a dinner of soft-shelled crabs. Suddenly a giant crab from the movie attacks me! No! I really wanted pizza!

I am in a supermarket and come to a pile of canned crabmeat. I take a can from the bottom and all of the cans fall down. The manager comes over and says, 'It's all right. Crabmeat has been going down lately.'

A general has undergone a brain transplant and has been given the brain of a crab. He orders a pincer movement against the enemy.

I meet Buster Crabbe in the subway and we have a discussion on the symbolism of Edgar Rice Burroughs's works. Buster is convinced that Burroughs was attempting to satirize Darwin.

Scientists discover that crab apples are the key to eternal life. Everyone eats them but me. I become a celebrity, the only man who will someday die.

I am marooned on a desert island with a beautiful girl. When I attempt to seduce her, she informs me that she has the crabs.

A baby crab in swaddling clothes is left on my doorstep. I take it in and raise it. I teach it many tricks and go on the Johnny Carson show. The crab pinches Johnny's mike and electrocutes itself.

The breeze is beginning to whip up now. The storm shall shortly be upon us. The clouds have already covered the sun and the sand is starting to cool off. Ah, the sand ...

A man is asleep on the beach. I recognize him as the man who introduced me to my wife. I quietly sneak up to him and pour a handful of sand down his throat and then run away.

I am timing an egg by a three-minute sand glass. The sand gets stuck and it is an hour before I notice it. My egg must be cut with a knife.

A juvenile delinquent pours sand into my gas tank. I am unable to go to the dentist.

I come home from bowling and find my wife in bed. Beside her is a man-shaped lump hiding under the covers. 'Who's there!' I shout. A dignified, fully-dressed man pops up and replies, 'Sander Vanocur, NBC News!'

A door-to-door salesman comes to my home. He is selling sand at thirty cents per bucket. 'It has many uses,' he informs me. 'A large quantity makes an effective shield against all alpha- and beta-rays and a large fraction of gamma-rays.' 'Do you know something I don't?' I query. Just then I see a brilliant flash and hear a distant roar. 'I'll take a hundred buckets,' I say.

A famous actor is on the set for his new movie when he hears a mystic voice warn, 'Move quickly!' A strong believer in psychic phenomena, he picks up a phone beside his chair, calls his real estate agent and puts his house up for sale. A second later, a large sand bag falls on his head, killing him.

I invite a hungry retarded person to my home. Placing a steak before him, I say, 'I expect you to polish this thing off in no time.' Obediently, he takes a piece of sandpaper from his pocket and begins doing so.

A pregnant child comes to my door on Halloween for a treat. I feel sorry for her and open a fresh box of cookies. 'Do you like Pecan Sandies?' I inquire. 'I do not like Pecan Sandies,' she replies, throwing a piece of sandstone through my bay window.

The rain hits! Ah, joyous! Splattering over my face, my arms, my legs! The smell of ozone in my nose delicious, ubiquitous, inspirational!

Leon Czolgosz stops at the Holiday Inn in Crab Creek, Maine, with his wife. He says to the manager, 'My wife is pregnant with a King of Kings and we need a room.' The manager queries, 'Are you Polish?' 'Yes,' Leon replies. 'You can sleep in the sand pit,' says the manager.

Leon Czolgosz and a sand inspector are observing the launching of a missile. The missile is pointed slightly askew as it rises. Quoth the sand inspector, 'That is a crab angle of three degrees.' 'Crab angle?' says Leon. 'Yes,' replies the other, 'the angle between the direction of movement of an airplane, rocket, or guided missile and the direction in which the nose points, resembling the sideways motion of a crab.' 'Ah,' says Leon, 'this curious expression involving crab is one I have never heard before.'

Noted naturalist Ivan T. Sanderson is attempting to dissect a live crab. Leon Czolgosz is standing at his side. 'Here, give me a hand, Leon!' pleads Ivan. Leon applauds.

A botanical expedition in search of a rare species of crabgrass is engulfed by a sandstorm. When the storm subsides, they inquire of a pastoral nomad, 'Is this the right way to the Czolgosz oasis?' 'No,' he replies, 'this is the way to Las Vegas. The other is due north.'

Leon is in a restaurant. He calls the waiter over. 'There is sand in my crabmeat,' he complains. The waiter has been waiting all day for this chance. 'Ha! Ha!' he laughs. 'Why, it's doing the *backstroke,* of course!'

Leon is out in the woods at night. He is lost. A skilled amateur astronomer, he recognizes the constellation of the Crab and walks with his eyes upward. He stumbles into a pool of quicksand and drowns.

Leon is rowing a boat off Sandy Hook, N.J. A Coast Guard cutter hails him. 'Hurricane Crabella is headed this way!' announces the captain. 'You'd better turn back to port.' 'No, thanks,' replies Leon. 'I have always preferred sherry.'

The rain is coming down harder now. All the bathers have left. Looking up, I see my five-year-old son, Dick, returning from the snack stand with an ice cream cone dripping all over his tightly clenched fist. Suddenly a bolt of lightning sears the air and strikes him, exploding in a great shock wave! All around his blackened body the sand is fused into a sort of natural glass. This curious effect of nature is one I have never seen before.

Fish Story

At 9 a.m. on his first day of work, young Mr. Jones knocked shyly on the open door of the Personnel Manager, Mr. Shad. 'Ahem. It's me sir.'

Mr. Shad looked up from his paperwork and focused his eyes thoughtfully. 'Oh, yes. It's ... Jones, is that right?'

'Yes, sir. You told me to report to you first thing.'

'Good! Splendid! Well, now, we'll begin by taking you around and introducing you to some of our key people. How's that?'

'Oh, that'll be swell, Mr. Shad.'

'Okay, follow me.' And out they went, down the hall. 'First, I'll introduce you to our Office Manager.'

They arrived at the Office Manager's office. Mr. Shad introduced them. 'Hello, Tom. I'd like you to meet Jones, our new design assistant. Jones, meet Tom Trout.'

'Welcome aboard, Jones.'

'Thank you, Mr. Trout.'

'I'm just taking Jones around,' explained Mr. Shad.

Mr. Shad then took him next door to meet the Director of Marketing. 'Pete, this young chap is Jones. Just starting today. Jones, this is Pete Bass.'

'How do you do.'

'How do you do.'

A little further down and across the hall, they stepped into the Traffic Supervisor's office. 'Al, this is Jones, who's starting with us today upstairs. Jones, this is Al Pike.'

'Nice to meet you, Jones.'

'My pleasure, sir.'

Mr. Shad then led Jones further down and around the corner to the office of the Sales Manager. 'This is Jones, our new employee in Design. This is our Sales Manager, Bob Crab.' They shook hands and exchanged courtesies.

Mr. Shad took Jones up to the second floor, where they found the Director of Public Relations at his desk. 'Hi. This is Jones, our new man in Design. Jones, this is our Director of Public Relations, Hank Salmon.'

'How do you do, Mr. Salmon.'

'Nice to meet you, Jones. Good luck with the new job.'

On their way out, Mr. Shad noticed a peculiar expression on the face of young Jones. 'Enjoying the tour, Jones?'

'Oh, yes, sir.'

'Good! Splendid! And now we'll meet the Advertising Director. Right in here. Here we are. Dave, I'd like you to meet Jones, our new design assistant. Jones, this is Dave Porgy.'

'How do you do,' said Jones.

'How do you do.'

'Just like *Porgy and Bess,* eh? Heh, heh,' said Jones with a nervous smile.

'I beg your pardon?' said Mr. Porgy.

'*Porgy and Bess,*' repeated Jones. 'It's a musical. I'm sure you've heard of it.'

'I'm afraid not,' said Mr. Porgy, not smiling.

As they left the office, Mr. Shad said to Jones, 'What was that crack about Porgy?'

'It's just, uh, you know, a musical.'

'I'm afraid I don't get the joke,' said Mr. Shad coldly. 'I was under the impression you needed this job.'

'Oh, yes, sir. I'm very sorry.'

Next, they met the Computer Systems Manager, whose name was Mr. Perch. After they walked out of his office, Jones could not suppress a nervous giggle. 'They're all fishes. Their names, I mean.'

Mr. Shad stopped. 'How's that?'

'Well, uh, I'm sure you realize everyone I've met so far has the name of a fish, heh, heh. No offense.'

'A crab is not a fish,' replied Mr. Shad in deadly earnest. 'It's a crustacean.'

'Oh ... Yes, of course,' said Jones, wilting under Mr. Shad's glare.

'Now, listen, Jones. You want to get off on the right foot with us, don't you?'

'Yes, sir.'

'Good. Splendid. A word to the wise is sufficient, as they say.'

They walked into another office. 'And this is our Stock Control Supervisor, Mr. Muskellunge. Mick, this is Jones, our new man in Design.'

'Glad to meet you, Jones.'

'Nice to meet you, sir,' said Jones glumly.

And on the next two floors they met, in rapid succession, Mr. Halibut, the Purchasing Officer, Mr. Stickleback, the Chief Accountant, Mr. Albacore, the Director of Overseas Trade, Dr. Carp, the company doctor, Miss Fluke, the company librarian, Mrs. Herring, the editor of the company magazine, Miss Hammerhead, the Customer Service Manager, Mr. Tarpon, the Comptroller, and Mr. Gourami, the Executive Director of Research and Development. After each meeting, Jones became increasingly withdrawn and upset.

They bumped into Mr. Turbot, the Executive Vice-President, in the corridor on the fifth floor.

'Mr. Turbot, this is Jones, the new man in Design.'

'How do you do, Jones.'

'Thank you,' said Jones vaguely, extending a limp hand and avoiding Mr. Turbot's eyes.

Mr. Turbot gave Mr. Shad a questioning look, as if to say *Where'd you dig him up?* 'Ahem, well, carry on, gentlemen,' he said, heading into his office.

Mr. Shad turned to Jones. 'That was the second most important man in the company.'

'Oh?'

'Yes, and I don't think he was too impressed.'

'I'm sorry.'

Mr. Shad put his hand on Jones's shoulder and gave him a fatherly look. 'Now, pick yourself up, lad. Don't let the first-day jitters get you. In this company, a new man is expected to be more ... you know, *dynamic*.' He made a little gesture with his clenched fist, suggesting strength. They began walking again, heading toward a large suite with a receptionist at a desk just inside the door. 'You have one more introduction and this is the one that counts the most, so try to make a good impression.'

'Yes, sir,' said Jones half-heartedly.

They stopped at the receptionist's desk. 'Is he in?'

'Yes, Mr. Shad. You can go right in. I'll just buzz him.'

They walked past her desk, turned down a short corridor, and stopped before a large door of highly polished wood with an ornate golden doorknob. Mr. Shad turned to the young man. 'Now, you'll meet the President. And let me tell you, he's as tough as nails and sharper than a barrel full of broken glass.'

'What's his name?' asked Jones, his eyes downcast.

'Wilson.'

'Wilson?' asked Jones, looking up with a smile of relief.

'Yes, Wilson.'

Jones straightened his tie and brushed back his hair. 'I'm ready!'

'Good! Splendid!'

Mr. Shad knocked, opened the door and marched in with his young charge.

The room was dimly lit with a diffuse greenish light coming from a huge aquarium that took up most of the room. An aerator gurgled and hummed peacefully, its bubbles tickling the fronds of underwater plants. The aquarium had all the usual trappings – the gravel, the plants, the rocks, the decorative sunken log, and the miniature deep-sea diver. A few little fish swam around, and a few snails clung to the glass sides. Suddenly, Jones froze with shock as a large fish – a black grouper – swam lazily out of the darker end of the tank to the side facing them and turned its cold-blooded gaze at the young man.

Mr. Shad spoke. 'Mr. Wilson, I'd like to present Jones, who is starting today in the Design Department.' He nudged Jones's elbow. '*Say something.*'

'H-h-h-how do you d-d-d-do, Mr. Wilson,' said Jones, swallowing hard as his stomach fluttered.

The black grouper's mouth opened slightly, and its lips pursed. Its fins moved slowly and gracefully as its eyes scanned Jones in jerky increments from top to bottom. The grouper's lips touched the glass and pursed again.

'Yes, sir!' said Mr. Shad. 'I think so, too!' He slapped Jones on the shoulder in a display of pride. 'I think he's going to work out fine, just fine! Well, we just wanted to stop by and say hello.' He nudged Jones. '*We're going. Say something.*'

'N-n-n-nice to have m-m-m-met you, Mr. Wilson,' he said, forcing a wan smile.

Mr. Shad steered him out of the office and closed the door behind them. The young man, shaking badly, gazed at the floor, transfixed with fright. 'Mr. Shad ... He's ... he's ...'

'Congratulations, Jones!' said Mr. Shad, pumping his hand and beaming with satisfaction.

'Huh?' said Jones, looking up.

'*He likes you!*'

The Hard-Working Garbage Men of Cleveland

' ... But the hand of the Lord was heavy upon them of Ashdod, and he destroyed them, and smote them with emerods, even Ashdod and the coasts thereof. The hand of the Lord was against the city with a very great destruction: and he smote the men of the city, both small and great, and they had emerods in their secret parts. And the men that died not were smitten with the emerods: and the cry of the city went up to heaven.' The mayor closed his book and glanced discreetly at his watch. 'Thank you, men.'

'Thank you, Mayor'

'Thank you, Your Honor.'

The grey-uniformed garbage men arose, prepared to face another day's work. The clatter of folding chairs mingled with the shuffling of shoes on the cement floor of the basement of the Department of Sanitation building.

Truck number 99 was much like any other, and its garbage men were much like any others. Garbage man Phil, 36 and married, had served as one of the prototypes for the popular children's book, *Garbage Men and Sewer Workers – What Do They Do?* Garbage man Joe, 28 and single, could answer almost any question about cheese. And garbage man Elrich, 31 and engaged, earnestly hoped to sire a son who would be as big and strong as the Golem.

By 9:15 truck 99 was on the streets. Joe drove the truck because he was an in-law of the city attorney, while Phil and Elrich loaded the garbage because they were not.

As Phil toted the familiar opaque green trash bags, now so popular, he thought about the old days, when people put their garbage in cans with lids. Phil would learn so many secrets by seeing what people put in their garbage. Indeed, it was hard to hide much from the neighborhood garbage man. Now the secrets were safely tied up, often in double or triple bags, as nervous men and women stood at living-room windows waiting to breathe a sigh of relief.

This morning, in addition to their collections, Phil and Elrich had a questionnaire to deliver to households in one of the better

17

neighborhoods. The questionnaire had only one question: 'What would you secretly like to eat?' With the questionnaire was given a stamped return envelope with only a post office box number on it.

At 11:00 they stopped at a corner where a man was waiting for them. He had an old briefcase, several pens sticking out of his shirt pocket, and a trace of white chalk on his fingers. Three folding chairs stood on the sidewalk. The man stood leaning against a light pole.

Phil, Elrich and Joe got out, sat down and took out pads and pens. 'Are there any questions concerning the previous material?' the man asked. They shook their heads. The man shuffled a few pages, cleared his throat and began:

'*The Third Heaven*.... The Holy Scriptures indicate that the third heaven is indeed a reality. It is the place where hangs the eternal world, the capital world of the universe, called Paradise. There is every reason to believe that the following features exist there:

'The most stately, eternally green trees of different varieties grace the terrain.

'The most nutritious and delicious fruits, vegetables, and nuts grow there without the need of poisonous fertilizers or chemical sprays.

'The most beautiful, exotic flowers of all colors grow there, along with the greenest, hardiest grass, more eternal than Astro-Turf.

'All birds sing beautiful songs – even the buzzard, the chicken and the ostrich.

'The land is watered by the purest rivers and springs, and the purest air blows there.

'The animals run and play together on the holy grounds in perfect harmony – the gorilla with the rabbit, the rhinoceros with the ant, and the hyena with the turtle.

'All is governed by Love and Reason. There is no crime or mental illness, no drugs or profanity, no hatred or fear. All is quiet and restful.' He looked at his three listeners and smiled. 'My, oh my! I'd love to live on that eternal planet, wouldn't you?'

'Yes.'

'Uh huh.'

'Right on.'

The man made a notation on his sheets. 'Kindly continue along in your study guides until the section *Elijah's Space Ride*. Are there any questions?' There were none.

18

The garbage men got up, folded the chairs for the instructor and put them in the trunk of his '52 Studebaker a few feet away. He got in and drove away. The garbage men resumed their collections until lunch time.

They had lunch at *Le Tournevis*, as was their wont. Pierre was happy to see them and gave them an excellent table. A lady who was in the restaurant for the first time remarked to Pierre, 'I didn't know you allowed bums to eat here. Look at the way they're dressed.'

Pierre gave her a sharp look. 'Madame, those gentlemen are municipal employees and a credit to their profession. They will always be welcome at *Le Tournevis*.' The lady felt ashamed and did not answer.

Phile ordered the *moustiquaire*. Joe ordered the *calcul biliaire au jus*. Elrich ordered the *fille de cuisine*. They did not drink wine, however, as wine affects the reasoning faculties.

Having restored their strength, the garbage men of truck 99 reported directly to a high school athletic field. Six florists from Akron were there waiting for them. They were thin, fragile-looking young men. A long rope lay on the ground.

Without speaking a word, the garbage men picked up one end of the rope, as the florists picked up their end. In between them was a mud puddle. They got a good grip and checked their footing. The school bell went off, and the teams strained at the rope. For an instant there was no movement, but then as one of the florists slipped, the garbage men got the rope moving their way and quickly pulled their adversaries into the mud. Then they walked back to the truck. That made it ten straight. Six Akron florists could never beat three Cleveland garbage men, a fact which readers of the *Plain Dealer*'s sports pages would be reminded of tomorrow.

The sanitation devotees continued their rounds until they reached the Poor Hospital around 2:30. While Joe and Elrich visited patients in the convalescent ward, Phil was led upstairs by the hospital director to a tiny private room where a man lay dying on the cleanest white sheets as a thin ray of light slanted across the room to touch his slippers.

'This one's ready to kick almost any time,' said the doctor in a low voice. 'Eighty-eight years old.'

'It's always a little hard to console the dying,' said Phil.

'Yeah, well, just ask him "How's things?" or "How's it going?" or whatever.'

'What's his name?'

'August Summerfield.'

Phil paused. He looked at the doctor, then at the white-haired man, who seemed to be napping peacefully. 'Not the famous one?'

'Yes, that's him. That's the man.'

'Jesus Christ, I'll be damned! That's the guy who wrote that filthy book.'

'Uh huh.'

'Son of a gun. Tsk.' Phil shook his head. He appeared hesitant. 'Frankly, I'm not in sympathy with smut writers. Not at all. We don't need guys like that. I read his book. I thought it was sick. So did my wife. Boy, I'll bet he goes to Hell.'

'Yeah, could be. Anyway, I can't give you a saint every time you come here.' He looked at his watch. 'I gotta yank out a kidney. Look, just say a few words to the old geezer. It's no big deal.'

'Sure.' Phil waited until the doctor left, closing the door behind him. He picked up a little wooden chair and brought it beside the bed. The sound caused the man's eyes to open. Phil would have preferred they hadn't.

The man mumbled. Phil leaned closer, and when he did, the man reached over and fastened on his arm with surprising strength. 'There is ... still ... so much ... to do,' he said. Phil stared at the man's hand, afraid to remove it. Summerfield was now gazing at the ceiling, focusing on its texture and patterns. He could remember as clearly as ever the streets of Paris in the thirties, where he had starved, where he had begged from strangers, where every little pain and joy was magnified a million times by his fevered mind, where world upon world was revealed to him in the reflection of a street light in a puddle, where every tree was a tree of Life, changing with the seasons for his eyes only. He thought of Kiki, for whom he waited almost every night in his threadbare coat and pathetic shoes but who never minded his appearance. No, Kiki had never found fault with him for anything. Even when he sketched her over and over and did it so badly, she always said it was beautiful. Kiki died of tuberculosis in 1938, and when he sat by her deathbed and sketched the most beautiful sketch of all, he cried because she would never see it ...

'Hey,' said Phil. 'Hey, Summerfield. Hey, I got a question. Just between you and me, heh heh. You ever fuck a nigger bitch? They any good?' He nudged the dying man, whose eyes were now closed and whose grip was relaxed. 'You still awake?' He decided the man was not. 'Aaa, what the hell,' he muttered, putting the man's hand back on the bed and getting up. He replaced the chair and left.

It was 3:00 and time for a little more garbage until the last job of the day. At 4:00 the garbage men stopped at Pavor Nocturnus Foods, Inc., the city's greatest canned food manufacturer. It was necessary to check on the production of the latest addition to P.N.'s proud line – P.N. Pork Brains in Milk Gravy.

Elrich was shown the actual canning and was fascinated to watch the shiny little cans whisk around in precise motions, receiving chopped pork brains here and a little milk gravy there, and then get sealed vacuum-tight.

Joe went up to Kardex to say hello to the clerks. They exchanged jokes and teases as Joe spot-checked their cards, making sure the arithmetic was correct. He also stopped to speak to the office supervisor, Mr. Myrmidon, and told him he hoped the company would change its mind about the computer because it would put so many nice people out of work. Mr. Myrmidon said it wasn't up to him.

And Phil was invited up to Advertising and Promotion. Anita Bryant was there, looking at the proofs for the magazine ads showing her at a picnic, surrounded by smiling children with plates of pork brains. The ad had her saying 'A day without P.N. Pork Brains is like a night without dreams.' The campaign would also include TV, billboards, and the modification of a small mountain in Idaho.

'Look at my charts,' said the marketing analyst, showing him several graphs on stiff paper with bold, blue lines straining up toward infinity.

'Gee,' said Phil, 'I always wanted to do some kind of work like this.'

'Aw, come on,' said the analyst, patting his arm. 'I think you ordinary guys get more joy out of life.'

Phil watched Anita out of the corner of his eye. She had her back to him and was bending over. *Those legs, those thighs, that ass ...* 'Yes, well ... keep up the good work. The mayor will be pleased.' The two shook hands.

Work was through for another day. Phil, Joe, and Elrich deposited their garbage at the Recycling Centre, returned their truck, picked up their enriched white bread from the dispatcher and headed for home. Phil especially felt fulfilled. He had worked hard, not only for the city of Cleveland but for his family. He was a good breadwinner, and it was a good life they had, all things considered.

As Phil sat on the bed that night, removing his socks and rubbing his sore feet, his wife said, 'Remember to call Mayor Perk at ten-fifteen. That's your new time.'

'Oh, yeah, right,' said Phil. It was 10:00. There would be just enough time to look up a good question for the mayor. He went to his encyclopedia, picked up Volume 'P' and opened it. He turned a few pages, then stopped, scanning a page. 'Nope, too easy,' he decided. He tried several other pages. 'Ah, this is good.' He smiled. He went back into the bedroom with the book. His wife was undressing. At exactly 10:15 he dialed the mayor's home phone. The phone rang only once. 'Hell, Mayor Perk? It's Phil ... Fine, sir and you? ... Okay, here we go.' He winked at his wife. 'Who succeeded Pope Clement VI?' A pause. He shook his head. 'Mayor, you're a brain. That's right ... I don't know how you do it ... Good night, sir.' He hung up.

Phil looked out the window of the weathered high-rise, not thinking anything in particular but merely feeling content. He watched the fat yellow moon sink into the haze over Lake Erie. His wife's reflection was there too as she readied herself. He pulled down the green shade. It was 10:30 and the day was done.

Now the night would begin.

The Discovery of Bismuth

Bismuth, from the German
wissmuth, or white mass; most
metallic member of its family,
which includes nitrogen,
phosphorus, arsenic,
antimony, and bismuth. It
melts at 271C but forms alloys
that melt as low as 47C; used
in electric fuses, solders, and
sprinklers. Its salts are used in
medicine and cosmetics. –
Hotcha.

It was a time when sunsets ran fast and rivers glowed bright. It was a time of torment and ecstasy, passion and vice, hope and despair, agony and sloth, mistrust and waste, amicability and procrastination, obstreperousness and confusion, violence and coexistence, nouns and conjunctions – in short, a time when logic and absurdity danced in a Motown frenzy aboard a ship fated for titanic disaster and a veritable tsunami of unleashed metaphors. In other words, a Thursday.

In such a time of travail did Liz Cerumen pant frantically at her kitchen table, her world torn asunder weekdays at three-thirty. The less-than-meteoric star of *Schoolmarm's Straits* had been novaed against her will and turned into a white dwarf – written out, kaput, and was about to be written out again. You'll see.

Overhead, a fleet of police planes zoomed helter-skelter, perilously close to the rooftops of this great, sprawling (or burgeoning, perhaps) midwestern metropolis, searching, observing, graphing. But they were not noticed by Eleanor, the pretty thirty-three and a half year old housewife, who sat at the kitchen table peeling rutabagas with reckless abandon.

She had tried to be faithful, but vice now held her in its grip. Life with The Oat had lost its alpen flavor. She thought back to the one she might have married. Yes, Sydney had become a success. He now owned a lucrative chain of El Syd's Teeno Latino Earth Underwear stores. But it was too late. Syd was gone.

After marrying The Oat, months passed like boring subway stations. Migrating birds went back and forth across her window. Then HE came into her life. It had happened so casually. She had gone to the Washday Problems Center to find out if anything would get out chromoplasm. There she was, at the end of the line for Qualitative Analysis – and then a flash of blue eyes, a flutter of excitement, an adrenalin chill and it was an accomplished fait accompli thing. She knew it. So did he. Bob would never understand. Neither would Jill.

Rutabaga husks were flung off in pained parabolas of anticipation as she looked at the clock. The handsome metallurgist would be here soon. The Oat would not be back till who knew when.

It was just like in *Schoolmarm's Straits,* thought Eleanor, but things like that *did* happen, and when you were in someone's nice story, moonbeams would wax and wane through the window and stars would speak to you, and then it was, oh, so sublime. Yes, she knew that when the cuckoo came out of the clock and asked for the public mandate for another hour, the famed pharmacologist would be here. She would look upon him with Mallomar-soft eyes, and he would dive straight through her windows open on the virgin forest of her mind as if falling through a fantastic country of late medieval blues and greens, coming at last to rest upon a lawn beside a fountain where a young girl in a white dress trimmed with pearls cradled in her lap the horned head of the lascivious unicorn without knowing what he represented. Teenagers in love knew this feeling well.

(Yet how could she have known that the 83rd element of the periodic table, chiefly found native in metaliferous veins associated with silver and cobalt, and which is also used in type metal, as I forgot to mention before, would be so pivotal in a tragedy that would be remembered throughout that small New England town long after *Schoolmarm's Straits* was but a slightly out-of-kilter neuron in the deep mausoleum of memory beneath the cerebral linoleum to which all flesh is heir?)

It seemed as though eons of time passed in Eleanor's mind before the doorbell rang.

'Good afternoon, ma'am. I'm selling lawn niggers.'

'What?'

'Lawn niggers.' He held one up. 'Looks great, huh?'

'I don't want any'

'Flamingoes? I got flamingoes?' He held one up.

'No, thank you.' She began to close the door.

'Wait! Wait! Wait! Just one more try, eh? Wait'll you see what I got.' He thrust his wrist toward her face. 'Star-Man watches.'

'I don't need a watch.'

'But this isn't a watch for telling time. It lets you do three things – fly through the air, detect radioactivity and speak Polish.'

'No, thank you.'

'I suppose you can already do those things, huh?'

'I beg your pardon?'

'Fly through the air and detect radioactivity and speak Polish.'

'You must be joking. I'm sorry, I'm busy.' She closed the door, but he slipped something under it. It was a ticket to the new hit play *Italian Frankenstein,* starring Tony Orlando and the late George Zucco.

Where was the famed toxicologist? Eleanor paced the floor, then turned on the TV.

'Before the end of the twentieth century, the scientists of Japan had succeeded in capturing all of the world's monsters and placing them on an island called Monster Land. There was Godzilla ... Rodan ... Yog ... Mothra ... Gamera ... and Granola ... The monsters were very happy there, for they had lots of food to eat, and the scientists could study them from an underground laboratory ...' Then it happened! Cities crumbled! Men ran! Women fainted! Terror reigned! Epidemics spread like plagues! All this and three commercials for Klong, the Wonder Facial For Today's With-it Pygmy Woman, came to pass before the late oxide hunter arrived.

'Oh!' she cried, 'I was so worried about you, my darling, my love,' and she smothered him with kisses.

'As I was saying on Monday,' he replied, 'I continued with my studies with C.W. Push College as a part-time student and in three years I got my master's degree in chemistry. Then for a year I took special courses in qualitative analysis and spectroscopy, and in five years went to the head of the Washday Problems Center.'

'Oh, Herschel, my everlasting love!' she sobbed.

'I continued studies leading to the PhD degree. It took me eight years of part-time study to do three of the four semesters, owing to the allotment of much of my time to waiting lists. For the past five years I have made no further progress.'

'You're hours overdue! I've been going crazy!'

25

'My tardiness was entirely due to the untimely passing of my brother, Wilfred, a civil servant assigned to telling stories to lost people in caves. He had no time to get out of the way of the stalagmite that snuffed out his life.'

'I'm so sorry, dear. How old was Wilfred?'

'He was thirty-four – too young to be killed by a stalagmite.'

While Eleanor wishfully hoped hopefully somehow, something, somewhere would effect a change in Herschel, she noticed his head jerk spastically and his fingers fold into a tight clench as his body stiffened. Herschel's eyes rolled back, then settled in the sagging lower lids as glossy black coals in a blazing fire. With a peculiar twist, he pursed his lips as if to speak, but only a prolonged hiss gargled from his throat, when his mouth drew back distorting his face to a serpent-like grimace, and his nostrils bulged as if laboring for breath in an arctic icy mist. 'Were Pinky Lee and Bruce Lee brothers?'

'Why, no, dear, I don't think so.' Tears hesitated at the interface of her lacrimal gland and whatever is right next to it. After all, she was every much a woman as any. Had hope fled? Every day a thud sounded in front of the house – the sound of her property values falling. She was thirty-three and a half – and getting older! And she felt that gnawing hunger that threatened to explode in torrents of hot, wet, frenzied ...

'As one would guess,' offered Herschel, 'affixtional endings do quite accordingly play an influential part in grammatical evaluation, and like words, much more so within context than out. In the statements *superfrantic renderings propagandize lustrous scintillations* or *beeble blooped blip,* a native of the language, for the most part, unconsciously realizes or inadvertently decides the words to be positioned in a correct order, in spite of probable lexical unfamiliarity, by the representations of affixtional signals positioned in a manner familiar to the language.'[1]

The gulp of air, ingurgitated by unexpected surprisal, compressed Herschel's tracheae to effect slight discoloration and the involuntary disruption of his nervous system brought about a sudden profusion of slimy sweat, as well as a writhing from fear of wetting his pants. When Herschel tried to give an explanation to his squirming hot flash, only the faintest squib ejected, so, to offset humiliation, he began reading. 'What's this? A religious tract?'

'The colors of the flying saucers depend upon the spiritual

---

1 I'm only kidding, there's no footnote.

mood of the saucer. Spiritual colors are easier to see at high altitudes. Therefore, pilots often see flying saucers. Those who climb high mountains may see them also. To others in the valley of the shadow of death, the saucers may appear white, as from alcohol or drugs. The poor saucers are afflicted just as people are. The poor alcoholic gets green men and so does the saucer. When the saucer gets full enough of green men and sick enough it lands, perhaps near a drunk who may be attractive to the devils. The green devils may say, 'Take me to your leaders,' and the drunk may say, 'Follow me,' and they do. Or, he may wave his bottle in the air and the green men may attack. Yes, to some of us there are dangers from flying saucers. However, that is not the Christian approach ...'

His reading was interrupted by Eleanor's ministrations to his feet. 'My darling, are your socks comfortable? I heard on the news about this hospital study on pain other than headache that socks pulling on foot hairs over a long period of time may lead to antisocial behavior, even insanity or violence.'

'Where was this study done?'

'At Canada Packers Institute. Oh, I do worry about you, my love.'

'I'm fine. Really.'

The noted cosmogonist wandered to the window, and down below on the sidewalk behind the enormous high-rise, a conversation was taking place:

'I'M AFRAID TO THINK ABOUT OUR NEXT GENERATION. THERE FUTURE IS VERY BLEAK. I PITY THE GOOD-PARENTS AND THERE OFF-SPRINGS. THE MOB HAS SOMETHING EVIL IN-STORED FOR THEM, BILL.'

'WHAT EVIL THING ARE YOU TALKING ABOUT, ROLAND?'

'DRUG'S TO DOPE THE CHILDREN WITH, BILL.'

'DRUG'S?'

'I'M TALKING ABOUT DOPE! IN THE FORM OF DRUG'S, BILL.'

'GOOD HEAVENS! OUR KID'S MIND WILL TURN THEM INTO A LIVING VEGETABLE. THEY'LL HAVE TO HAVE DRUG-CENTERS ON EVERY STREET TO COPE WITH THIS TERRIBLE HABITUAL-DRUG, ROLAND.'

'I KNOW BILL,' SAID ROLAND RATHER GLOOMY.

'HOW CAN A HUMAN-BEING SINK SO LOW, AS TO DESTROY HIS OR HER OWN LIFE AS WELL AS OTHER HUMAN BEINGS, WHEN GOD INTENDED A HUMAN-LIFE TO GROW AND LIVE, ROLAND.'

'WHAT THE HELL DOES THE MOB CARE ABOUT HUMAN-LIFE? NOR DO THERE FAMILIES, THERE RELATIONS AND ALL THOSE OTHER PARISITES WHO DON'T GIVE A DAM ABOUT YOUR KIDS OR MINE, WHEN THERE KIDS WILL BE THE SELLERS OR PUSHERS IN THE TRAFFIC OF DRUGS, BILL.'

'BROTHER I SURE LEARNED A LOT ABOUT LIFE, CRIME, AND THE MOB JUST WALKING ALONG THIS SIDE-WALK WITH YOU, ROLAND. WHAT LIFE I SAW WAS THROUGH A PAIR OF ROSES-COLORED GLASS'S, ROLAND.'

'I THINK THAT TRUCK IS GOING TO HIT US, BILL.'

Just then the phone rang. It was Caldo Clistere, the famed emcee of *Jackpot Nigger Bingo*, asking if Eleanor could name any five Emory University professors who danced well and loved children, in return for which she would win a sum of money large enough to allow her and Herschel to leave this story and settle in a green pasture. However, she couldn't, so they didn't.

She *might* have looked at Herschel, eyes downcast, soul far away, as if to say, 'You know, you're not helping the editor make sense of this. He's trying to do his job to the best of his ability.'

'Phooey!' Herschel *might* have ejaculated. 'He probably hasn't even gotten this far.'

It would have been true. These very words were not even being read by many loathsome, inadequate and pockmarked editors who came here from other countries to take away the rightful jobs of our citizens in asylums, but they don't know I'm saying all this because they sent it back around the point that the police planes zoomed helter-skelter.

Herschel instead elaborated: 'The seminal causes of Pater's early and constant suspicion of absolutist philosophical systems lie buried somewhere in the obscurity of his formative years at the Haunted Strangler Prep School and in the rational historicism he inherited from Burckhardt and Michelet, which was later confirmed by his reading of Hegel and Darwin. They need not concern us. It is enough to state that after patient study of all philosophical alternatives rehearsed in the quasi-autobiographical *Marius the Epicurian*, Pater admitted the improbability, or at best the incognitivity, of any reality which cannot be proved by empirical verification.'[2]

'Herschel,' Eleanor pleaded, 'listen to me. Did you get your divorce?'

2 Uhlan, Edward. *Walter Horatio Pater: Minnow Among the Whales*, Hicksville, New York: Exposition Press.

'Yes,' the famed cosmetologist answered. 'Ester had become estranged from me for several years, and I could not bear to live with a strange woman. Of course, she is collecting antimony.'

'You do ... care for me, don't you, Herschel?'

He regarded her fulsome figure, so rich, palatable and organic. 'Why, yes.'

'Then take me!' she screamed, clutching at his white lab smock. 'Feel my hot, womanly flesh! For eight long years my flesh has known no joy! I would lie awake so many nights in hot flashes and / or cold chills, my hungry body wanting a long, hard plenum! I stayed away from church – me, a devout Baculite – because I knew I might confess my sinful state of mind! Eight years, do you hear me? Oh, how could you know when we first met what kind of awful fantasies danced in my mind! But I can't help it, I tell you! I need what only you can give me! Surely, you can understand that as a man of maturity and experience!'

'You are visiting your parents in Cincinnati? I shall be happy to furnish transportation to the airport. I have enjoyed watching airplanes since the age of five years old. The development of air travel has made possible the standard of living and many of the modern comforts we enjoy today.'

Suddenly, there was the sound of feet wiping on the welcome mat outside the front door, and an accompanying whistling of the poignant Wagnerian song, *Ich möchte diese Schuhe putzen lassen.*

'Quick,' she said to the celebrated biophysicist. 'It's my husband! Go out the back door!' She shoved him into the kitchen and out the door, and came back into the living room, trying to regain her composure as The Oat was hanging his cape in the closet. He wore red boots, brown leotards, and matching top with an orange O on the chest. The Oat had become pot-bellied with middle-age.

'How was work, dear?' said Eleanor with forced calm.

'Okay,' said The Oat. 'I had to go to Monster Land to save Kimiko and Kazuo. Finished up around 3:30. Boy these socks are hurting me!' He took off his boots and pulled his socks off, rubbing his hairy feet. 'Say, before I forget, I want you to call the printer tomorrow and tell him the business cards have to be done over. Can't go around handing out cards that say "The Oaf."'

Make conversation, look natural, she told herself. 'Um, you missed a nice episode on *Schoolmarm's Straits.*'

'I hate that program. Bunch of idiots. So what happened?'

'Mildred's baby was born in the post office, and she couldn't pay the special delivery charge, so they kept it there and said they'd send it around fourth class, and then –' *Oh, no! What's that on the floor?*

'Uh huh.' He straightened up. Then something caught his eye. 'What's that?' He picked up a lump of metal. Eleanor froze. The Oat examined it, felt its weight, sniffed it, tasted it. 'It's bismuth, isn't it? ISN'T IT? IT'S BISMUTH!'

'No!'

'DON'T LIE TO ME. HE'S BEEN AROUND AGAIN, HASN'T HE?'

She screamed, for a look of insane fury came over him.

'HERE IS A GUN! I SHOOT YOU!' BANG!

'Oh, I die!'

And so a great discovery was paid for in full by the sacrifice of a noble life. Now sprinklers give life to new sod in the suburbs, fuses sustain the air conditioners of Kansas, typesetters prepare these words, and our upset stomachs are quickly relieved. For all these things, dear God, we kneel and give thanks.

Filling Orders in Albania

I was proud to be the first order filler in Albania. George, my foreman, said we'd be a great team. He was the first foreman in Albania.

From the window of the third-floor stockroom in downtown Tirana, he gestured with a sweep of his arm. 'Albania used to be great. Now it's not so great. But we make it great once more.'

Our first order came up the pneumatic tube. George took it out and unfolded it with official care. 'Ahem, let's see. Ah, yes. It's from Peter Gamoukian's General Store, our best customer – so far. Here. You fill it. I supervise.'

I took the order with a little wooden cart stolen from the post office and headed for the correct row of bins. The sound of the defective wheels set a little song going in my head, which I am proud to say I made up with no help at all:

Filling orders in Albania
It's a new kind of mania
Filling orders in Albania
Yeah, yeah, yeah.

My order sheet had been processed by the first Kardex clerk in Albania and put through the first computer in Albania. It read as follows:

    1 goatskin
    1 belt
    1 shoo polish
    1 cheez
    1 bred
    1 rock, big
    2 cloth, green
    1 gun, 45

Luckily, there was exactly the right amount of merchandise in the bins, except for the gun. 'George, there is no gun.'

George coughed. 'Oh, really? We must be out of stock. Just mark it "O.S." and we back-order it.'

I wheeled the cart back and packed the goods in a cardboard carton. George supervised my every move. 'You do good work. I tell the agency they send me a good order filler.' I smiled. He went on, 'Ah, yes, someday Albania be great again. Soon I bring two girls from my village – one for you and one for me. In a few generations, we have a master race.' I felt historical.

'Any more orders to fill?' I asked.

'Not yet. Business slow at first but maybe better tomorrow. Here. You deliver the carton. We have no shipper. Number forty-five, Alley of the Jackals. Tell Peter Gamoukian hello from me. Come right back.'

I was out the door and in the street in no time, my blue order filler's uniform and cap still crisp and new beneath the mid-summer sun. Bearded men slipped furtively into shadows and women disappeared into shops as I walked along. A slow-moving truck, loaded with the latest hybrid non-clucking chickens, passed me. I saw a crate stenciled 'P. GAMOUKIAN, 45 ALLEY OF JACKALS.' I jumped on the back and watched the main street roll itself out beneath my feet like an old, drab carpet.

The hum of the motor and the noise of the slightly defective wheels made me think of my little song. I turned to the silent chickens and sang to them softly:

Filling orders in Albania
It's a new kind of mania
Filling orders in Albania
Quack, quack, quack.

Office Worker's Dreams

Modern Facilities

When I ask in the office where the men's room is, the middle-aged secretary tells me it's upstairs 'under the sign, almost directly overhead.' I go upstairs and find the second floor to be an empty framework of wooden beams, like a house under construction. In the corner I see a sign:'MEN.' There is nothing under it. No toilet. No door. Nothing. I am greatly disturbed but must relieve myself immediately. I look around. Am I to do it here? Is this what is done in this company? I've never seen such a thing before. I look at the floor and see that it is wet. There is a smell of urine. Apparently, this is where men relieve themselves! Astonishing! What is also astonishing is that there are cracks between the floor boards. I can see the office where I was a minute ago. The women are at their desks right below me. The secretary who directed me is smoking a cigarette and coding orders. I can wait no longer! I unzip myself and after a moment of self-consciousness, I being to release a strong, healthy stream of piss. It spatters warmly on the floor. Then I hear a voice scream, 'Jesus Christ! There's piss coming down through the ceiling!' An uproar spreads through the office, but I can't stop. The piss goes on and on and on! I hear footsteps from across the floor. It is the president of the company, leading a prospective client by the arm. I hear him say, 'I want to assure you we have the most modern facilities.'

Term of Employment Determined By Pens

I report to work ten minutes early, as my supervisor has requested. He shows me which desk I am to occupy. Then he hands me an attractive pen – the opaque, non-retractable kind.

'I am not only the Supervisor but also Central Pen Control. Here is your first pen. It is the only kind of pen you may use, and you may only use it here at the office. Under our rules, you cannot quit your job until your pen runs out of ink. If your pen *does* run out of ink, you will be fired if you cannot obtain a new one. There are twelve employees in this office. Each one has been given a pen.

33

Each employee may obtain one replacement pen from me every two months but no more than five during any calendar year, and he may obtain a replacement under this provision even if his pen has not run out of ink. Also, I hide twelve pens in various secret places in the office on the first of the year and one additional pen on the first of each month. Now, it is possible to possess more than one pen, but all pens are not necessarily full. Since they are opaque, you cannot be sure how much ink is left. Also, these pens have a special design and serial number so that you can't go to a store and buy them. You can only get them from me, and it is impossible to steal them. Pens may be bought and sold among employees. If you lose your pen, you'd better find one or buy one, or you can get one from me if it's been more than two months. Now, to avoid theft, you get your pen from your pen locker in my office in the morning and deposit it there at the end of the day. Persons finding hidden pens, however, are not required to declare them but usually do in order to make them available for sale, sometimes for fifty dollars or more. Also, spare pens acquired in this manner invariably remain in the office because the person would want it as insurance in case he lost his. Now, if you want to leave your job, you must not have any spare pens left. You cannot sell them just to be able to leave, but you can sell your spares and then wait till the one you have runs out of ink. Now, some employees like to trade pens for fun since no one knows which is fuller, but you have to watch out for some of these tricksters who look for the first indication of a pen's running dry and then trade it off on an unsuspecting employee. However, if you *want* to leave your job, you might want to acquire such a pen, sell your others, and then let the near-empty pen run out on you. Now, one thing I don't allow is scribbling on a pad to make your pen run out. That ink was put there to do useful work. Another thing you cannot do is hold a dry pen. You must declare it to be dry and give it to me for disposal. I have the right to check every pen on your person to see that it still works. One other thing is making small marks on pens to indicate their age, which is okay and legal. Many employees like to do that when they find a pen or get a new one from me. For instance, they make one scratch for January, two for February, and so on. This way, pens in circulation are of a known age, but of course they may not have been in use continuously. And under the scratch system it is easy to add scratches to make the pen seem newer and thus make it more valuable to sell. Now, in the case where a pen is damaged by being sat on or melted on the hot plate ...'

The Impact of Goodness

I am opening the morning mail while my boss is in his office with the door closed. The light on my extension phone tells me he is busy making more big deals. From these run-down offices on top of a luncheonette, he operates numerous businesses: Youth-Aid Health Products, Lucky Charms, the Correspondence College of Song-Writing, Sub-Arctic Land Developments, the International Theosophy Institute, Madame Zena (Spiritual Counselor), Save The Children of Fernando Po, the Contest-Lovers Club, and Dr. Goodman's Marital Aids. And those are the ones I *know* about.

I separate the day's receipts into folders – one for each business. Complaints are set aside for him to glance at and then throw out. Utility bills, dunning notices from suppliers and printers, and letters from various consumer and government agencies go into yet another folder marked 'No Reply Necessary.'

Today, an unusual letter has come in the mail, along with a $15.00 cheque made out to Youth-Aid. It is from a Mrs. Everson or Emerson or something like that, in a nursing home in Mississippi. The handwriting is extremely shaky, but it seems to read:

Dear Sir:

Awhile back I sent a check for $30.00 for the 3 ounce jar of Miracle Youth Cream ... (illegible) ... got the 6 ounce jar instead. In your ad it says the 6 ounce jar is $45.00. Now I am ... (illegible) ... keep it or return it ... (illegible) ... send you the difference of $15.00.

A very happy customer,

Mrs. A. Everson (?)

I put this letter on top of the Youth-Aid mail. I want my boss to see it first. He's sure to find it amusing. I take all the folders, knock gently on the door, let myself in, and place the folders before him on the desk. He is on the phone, saying to someone, ' ... just the way we did in L.A. The contractor digs the hole and disappears, and we split the customer's money ... Yeah ... Exactly ... What can they do? Nothing ... '

I return to my desk and browse through the newspaper.

Five minutes later, I hear his door open. He comes out, tears streaming down his face. He has Mrs. Everson's letter and cheque in his hand. Voice cracking, he says to me, 'Thank God ... there is still ... some honesty ... left in this world!'

35

Upward Mobility

My throat dry, I knock on the Sales Manager's door. I hear him bark, 'Come in!'

I enter and close the door behind me. Mr. Allen is smoking one of his fifty-cent cigars although it is only 9:30 in the morning. The sleeves of his white shirt are rolled back. There is a plain, white towel on his desk blotter. 'Sit down.' He beckons me to the chair beside his huge mahogany desk. The desk and shelves are cluttered with expensive accessories. Behind him are the large framed photos of his severe-looking father and his even severer-looking grandfather.

'Move your chair around here. Don't be shy,' he says with a wink. His shoes and socks are off, his trousers are rolled up. There is a basin of grey, soapy water on the floor. I am now sitting directly facing him behind the desk. My tie is choking me.

He blows a stream of smoke vertically by curling his lower lip. 'I hope you know I'm giving you the first shot at moving up to a better territory.'

'Thanks, Mr. Allen. It's more than I expected.'

'Your sales figures are good. More than I thought possible for the Yukon.' He grins. 'Feel lucky?'

'I don't know.'

'Okay, have a go at it.' I hesitate. 'Go ahead. They're clean.'

I lean down and look at his two newly washed feet. Each of his toes represents a different territory, but I have no way of knowing which. I am required to pick one of his toes ... and put it in my mouth.

Steeling myself, I separate his left little toe slightly and put my lips around it. Then I look up and await the verdict.

He laughs, tapping the ash of his cigar. 'Hoo! Hoo! Oh, boy! Jesus, do I feel sorry for you, ha ha! You picked the same lousy territory!'

'NO!'

'Jeez, I'm sorry, Phil.' Then he leans forward confidentially and puts his hand on my shoulder. 'Your shyness worked against you. You thought the smallest toe would be the least unpleasant.' I nod. 'My boy,' he continues, giving me a pat of encouragement, 'if you want to advance quickly in the world of business, you must not be afraid to take the boss's big toe in your mouth and suck on it.'

36

Organic Sense

I am sitting at a desk by a window facing a crumbling brick building and an alley full of garbage. I am stuffing envelopes with a Gestation Table For Domestic Animals. They are being sent to a mailing list of persons responding to a magazine ad (*LONELY? LIKE TO GET MAIL? TEN DOLLARS BRINGS YOU INTERESTING MAIL FOR LIFE!*).

When my supervisor comes by, I give him the batch just completed. Then I say, 'Excuse me, sir, but I think you should know these gestation tables are all wrong. I just noticed. They must have got scrambled at the printer's or something.'

'Oh, really? How do you know?'

'I did two years of animal husbandry at Michigan State. Here, take this for example. The gestation and incubation period for a buffalo – twenty-seven days. Obviously that's not right. It's more like two hundred and seventy days.'

'Did you finish your degree at Michigan State?'

'No, I just did two years.'

'Well, then, I'd go by the table as it is.'

'Are you kidding? Do you think a buffalo can give birth in twenty-seven days?'

'It's not for me to say. I'm just the mailroom supervisor.'

'But–'

'Just keep doing what you're doing and don't worry about it.'

'But it's wrong.'

He sighs, then leans against my desk. 'All right, look, even if it is wrong, there's nothing I can do about it. I just do what they tell me.'

'Then how will it ever get straight?'

'Well ... ' He hesitates. 'These things get straightened out eventually. There are self-correcting processes out there in the world for things like this. Like, for instance, a guy expects to have a baby buffalo in twenty-seven days, and it doesn't come. So he knows something's wrong. And maybe some other people realize the same thing. So they tell their friends about it, and their friends decide not to send away for our stuff. Then – '

'Hold it. What friends? This stuff goes to people who are lonely. They can't have too many friends.'

He shifts his weight to the other foot. 'Well, I mean the few friends they *do* have, or just neighbors at least. The word gets around that the numbers on the table are wrong. So we get fewer orders for our mailings. Then the bosses downstairs start to wonder and maybe call in some marketing experts, and how those experts find out about the buffalo I don't know for sure, but believe me, they do. So then, after we use up these few million tables, they'll have new ones printed with the right numbers. And the important thing is we don't get in any hot water.' He taps the envelopes into a neat stack. 'You see, the world corrects itself, just like an organism. It has what you might call an organic sense.'

After he walks away, I sit back in my chair and look out my filthy window. Through the grime, I see a drunk has made himself comfortable amid the garbage. Above, the sky is dark enough for rain. At least, it looks that way.

The Poem That Changed the World

It was upon my return to Earth after a mission to reorganize all the libraries of the Magellanic Clouds that I was told all that had happened. My friend Gus, who picked me up at the spaceport, said, 'I'm sure you've heard the gossip about the big changes on Earth.' I said I had heard some rumors – nothing that made sense, however. 'Well, let me tell you,' he went on, 'you have to see it to believe it! It's greater than I would have thought possible! It's utterly fantastic! To think that a poem, *a mere poem* ... '

'Watch it, you're tailgating,' I interrupted, as we came up quickly on the vehicle ahead.

'Oh, sorry. Wasn't paying attention. Anyway, as I was saying, to think that a poem could change the world so completely ... Why, it's Utopia come true, nothing less!'

'Well,' I mused, 'I suppose it's possible – in theory, that is. The power of words and ideas and all that. Maybe the time was right. The right poem at the right time, you know what I mean?'

'Yes, yes, I think that's it. What else?'

The access highway was always busy at this time of day as scores of flights were landing. We found ourselves at a bottleneck. As two lanes of traffic merged, drivers called out to each other helpfully:

'Go ahead!'

'After you!'

'Please, I insist!'

'Thank you, you're most kind!'

'It's a pleasure!'

'You see?' said Gus. 'Just one of the many changes. People are so much more polite than before. They understand the importance of cooperation, of neighborliness. They have a new perspective. That's it – *a new perspective. And new values!'*

I sat in silence, trying to grasp the very idea of it. It was hard. After a minute or so, I asked Gus to turn on the radio.

'Sure thing. All the news is good these days.'

Click. ' ... And here are the top headlines of the hour ... Pope

Calls Ecumenical Conference a Success ... The Nation's Divorce Rate Plummets to Almost Zero ... Native Peoples Attribute End of Alcoholism to Poem ... And Ellsworth Gortz Wins Nobel Peace Prize ...'

'That's him!' Gus broke in excitedly. 'Ellsworth Gortz! He wrote The Poem!'

As we entered the core of the city, I was impressed by its exceptional cleanliness and tranquility. There was not a speck of litter to be seen. The old hustle and bustle were gone. A relaxed, carefree tone seemed to pervade the environment. It was Saturday night. Well-dressed, well-groomed teenagers strolled along, exchanging pleasantries with their elders. The souped-up cars I used to know had given way to modest, fuel-efficient vehicles and bicycles. Crowds were lined up to hear poetry readings in what used to be taverns and strip joints. The video arcades had closed for lack of business and were supplanted by chess clubs. Lovely trees throve even in the heart of the city, and songbirds filled the air with their sweet notes.

'The cops don't wear guns any more,' Gus informed me. 'Crime practically no longer exists. The new perspectives, the new values. People know how to live socially now.'

'Right.'

'... Thanks to the Poem," I said.

'How about the economy? Inflation? Unemployment? Strikes?'

'That's all over with. People have learned to derive joy from any sort of work, however menial. Money is a low priority. People are content with what they have. And all prices have been frozen by common agreement. It's so much simpler that way, don't you agree?'

'I certainly do. By the way, who's in power, the Liberals?'

'The Liberals? Boy, are you out of date! All the parties merged into one and became the Harmony Party.'

'Then who's the Opposition?'

'Opposition? What is there to oppose?'

'You've got me there,' I conceded. Then I thought a moment. 'Corruption? Scandals? Conflicts of Interest? Red tape? ... Okay, quit laughing, Gus.'

We were stopped at a red light. A family of East Indians crossed the street in front of us, dressed in their traditional clothing. 'How about prejudice?' I ventured. 'There will always be prejudice.'

'Not any more,' he replied, shaking his head.

'Good Lord! You don't mean it!' I was flabbergasted.

'The new values and perspectives have changed everyone and everything – fundamentally.'

'But how could a poem reach so many people? Hardly anyone reads poetry.'

'The Poem has been broadcast on every radio and TV station every day in every country. In this country, they even sign off with it at the end of the day, before the national anthem. It's been run in every newspaper. It's been up on billboards. They give copies away free in the post office. Children recite it in school every morning. And credit card companies even print it on the back of their bills.'

'Incredible! What was the poet's name again?'

'Ellsworth Gortz.'

'*Ellsworth Gortz,*' I repeated, savoring each syllable on my lips like some exotic foreign food. 'But who is he? I mean, where did he come from?'

'He was just a nobody, really. Just another starving poet. Then somebody got hold of The Poem. He always said he had only one good poem in him and that was it.'

'It only takes one, I guess.' Gus nodded his agreement. I looked at him. 'Okay, when do I get to read The Poem, or hear it?'

Gus smiled. 'Very soon. In fact, you'll not only get to read it, you'll get to meet Gortz himself. He lives in my building and that's where we're going!'

I was thrilled! I was actually going to meet the man who wrote The Poem!

We passed a theater marquee with the title *The Ellsworth Gortz Story.* A parcel of prime downtown land had been cleared for the erection of a Gortz monument. The city's main street had been renamed Gortz Street.

Outside Gus's apartment building, girls of all ages clustered around the front door as the doorman kept shooing them away. Some of them were in tears. 'Ellsworth! Ellsworth!' they screamed. 'I love you! I want your baby!'

Gus remarked, 'Gortz has the best sex life of any man I know.'

'Well, I guess that's what happens when you write a great poem.'

Riding up in the elevator, Gus said, 'To get back to what I was saying before, The Poem has been translated into every known language. After the translation into Russian, the Russians granted complete autonomy to their satellites and abandoned the arms race. They finally understood the meaning of life and the importance of freedom and love in a way that Karl Marx could never explain. They saw the Light, in other words.'

'Wonderful!'

'After The Poem was translated into Arabic and Hebrew, the Arabs and Jews literally fell on each other with brotherly love, and the P.L.O. threw down their weapons. Now it's peace and harmony.'

'Leave it to new perspectives every time.'

'When The Poem was translated into Italian, the Mafia and the Red Brigade dissolved themselves. The Italian government is now stable and the lira is one of the strongest currencies in the world. In India, the population explosion has been stemmed by the translation of The Poem into all the Indian dialects, and all vestiges of the caste system have been abolished. The Chinese translation has resulted in a democratic regime there, and all of Southeast Asia has become stable. As for Africa, well, the bad old days are gone. Tribal warfare is over, the agricultural economies are all viable, and the elephants are no longer in danger of extinction.'

The door opened on the 85th floor, where Gortz occupied three adjoining apartments. The building's management wanted to make sure he had enough room to feel comfortable and enjoy peace and quiet. He lived there rent-free. They considered themselves honored to have him as a tenant. Moreover, their new sense of values had led them to make at least fifty of their best apartments available rent-free to other struggling poets and artists.

Gus knocked on the door to 85B. We heard footsteps cushioned by thick carpeting coming toward us. Then the door opened, revealing Ellsworth Gortz. He was short, fat, pimply, incredibly ugly, and reeked of sweat, bad breath, and tobacco. His thick beard was full of crumbs and other food matter and his teeth were crooked and discolored. His hands were filthy, his clothing was soiled and wrinkled, and his bare feet had the most disgusting toenails I had ever seen. 'Oh, hi, Gus,' he said.

'Hi, Ellsworth. I brought my friend Zack to meet you.' Gortz and I shook hands. 'Zack's been away to the Clouds and just got back today. He doesn't even know your poem yet.'

Gortz chuckled. 'Come on in!' We stepped in. The place was a veritable pig sty. He turned to two gorgeous young girls sitting on the couch. 'Girls, go get us something cold to drink, okay?' They went into the kitchen, giggling. Gortz turned back to me. 'Well, Zack, you may be the only grown person on Earth who hasn't seen The Poem.'

'I guess so.'

'I've got it in the next room. Come on.' We followed him, stepping carefully among piles of garbage, food wrappers, laundry, junk, and old cat litter until he had gotten us into a darkened room. He closed the door behind us. 'Now watch,' he said. He switched on an ultra-violet light, and the lines of phosphorescent paint on the wall burst forth in multi-colored brilliance! This was it! – the poem that had changed the world:

Death Probes Absurdity
by Ellsworth Gortz

Stimulations come from
The heavens,
The three revelations of God,
The stars, the moon, and the
Sun.
The greatest form of creation
Is energy,
As I know life, the electro probes
Dynamate the nervous system,
Thus, gas flows freely.

Built up gas fuses and explodes
Thus, statured being man is
Unlimited,
And gas built up
Causes heart failure.
So run, walk, scream
From your whole being,
And let loose that gas.
Relieve all self made
Tension,
Hold nothing back.

Waiting for Halley's Comet

I'm downtown waiting for my pen pal, Richard Oelze, and somehow I sense exactly what is happening.

An accountant around the corner is waiting to appear in a magazine called *Accountants Worth Watching*.

A civil servant in the bank tower is gathering his courage to tell his supervisor that he would like a new chair. He was promised a new chair two months ago. Where is it?

A terrible band called *The Bavarian Night Bugs* is waiting to find work.

An ad copywriter behind a tinted window in the distance is waiting for inspiration to write a jingle for Nebo Nails. He can't think straight because he's wondering how things will go with his wife tonight. All he has so far is:

hammer them down
they won't make you frown
hammer them in
then you will grin.

He crumples the paper and throws it in the wastebasket.

In the second-floor warehouse across the street, there is a clot of dust behind a bin, which has not been touched for eleven years. An order filler looks at it every day, and his resentment grows. Meanwhile, the janitor is waiting to be appreciated.

An inventor buying peanuts at the corner is waiting to hear from the company to whom he sent his idea for a Braille television. It's just a matter of time, he believes, before he revolutionizes communications for the blind.

An inmate in the mental health center is waiting for a red Corvette in the lot across the street to be sold. When this happens, it will be a sign to him from God.

An astrologer is waiting for Mars to leave Virgo.

Andy Varipapa goes by on the streetcar. He sticks his head out the window and says to me, 'Hey, I got a new trick! Wait till you see it!'

An old Jew who survived Auschwitz is waiting for the gas company to restore his gas. They are waiting for his cheque to clear.

A manager trainee in Woolworth's is waiting to get rid of Easter candy, folding chairs, and shoes made in Poland.

A man way up in the Belvedere Apartments has a high-powered rifle aimed at the parking lot. He is waiting for the poodle that always pisses on the tires of his Cadillac.

Fred of Fred's Esso is waiting for valve stems.

A girl who is afraid of dentists is waiting for the pain to go away by itself.

A young artist refuses to paint until his girlfriend calls him.

A postman is forming the Natural Fiber Party. His goal is to enact legislation restoring the natural fiber to food, thus curing constipation, the root cause of all human inefficiency. He is the only member so far, but in ten or twenty years, the NFP should swing a lot of weight.

In a bachelor apartment on top of Nick's Lunch Box, an old and faithful office worker who was retired yesterday after fifty years lies in bed looking at his gold watch and waits to die.

An Italian woman with a whining brat has just bought a $150 curse from a gypsy to make her neighbor choke to death on a shrimp.

A teenage dropout is waiting to hear from Johnny Cash. He sent Johnny his 'new hit song,' *Yunga Bunga Doo Doo Boy.*

A housewife is waiting for her husband to leave the house.

Beverly is waiting for Ted in the Holiday Inn.

Two men in a black Mustang are waiting for the security guard to go for coffee.

Twenty-three junior executives within a 100-yard radius are waiting for authorization.

An unemployed axe-grinder is waiting for gas to hit a dollar a gallon so he can fill up his van, crash through the front door of an oil company, and cause a big fire.

Across the street and down the block a little, on the top floor of a tenement, is a man waiting for the return of Halley's Comet. He has a 'countdown calendar' on his wall and tears off a day at a time. All his years of suffering will be worth it when the comet comes back to shine in the sky and lift men out of their misery. No one else could possibly understand what it means to him, what he feels in his heart, except maybe for *her.*

He thinks of the girl he once knew so long ago. If he still knew her, if he knew where to find her, he would take her out to a high meadow to see the return of Halley's Comet. He would show her all the wonders of the night sky and tell her the original myths of the constellations. There would be a warm breeze and night smells such as cannot be remembered but only experienced. Her hair must be longer now and certainly no less red, and she would still be as beautiful as before. His entire life would come down to that single moment, when there would be nothing left to wait for, when all would be fulfilled.

From his tenement window, the man's dreamy gaze limps along the street to rest at the bench where I'm sitting, and for a second our eyes meet.

Teleological – With Chicken Meat

Larry Norton's Recollection
I was up from Tidewater only two weeks. It was really a thrill, something I was hoping for for a long time. You know, rubbing shoulders with Seaver and Jones and Harrelson and the rest of those guys. I didn't really expect to play regular, but then Boswell got sick and I got into the line-up. It was really swell, you know? I was kind of nervous and all. It seemed like there was a million people in the stands and there I was standing at the plate facing Ferguson Jenkins. It was the bottom of the fifth and we were down six to nothing already. I'd been keeping my eyes on the sky for about the past inning or so. It looked pretty dark and I thought sure the rain would start coming down any second. I was up with two outs and all I could think of was stalling around, rubbing my hands with dirt and all that. I was praying so hard for it to rain before the inning was over, you know? I kept thinking RAIN! RAIN! RAIN! so hard I though my head would break open. I was afraid to even swing at the ball. Jenkins had me two and two, and he was in a hurry to get one more by me.

Just then there was a tremendous roar of thunder right over us. Any second, I thought. It's really going to pour any second. Jenkins went into his wind-up and it was right then that it hit him on the head and he stopped. Then it was coming down all over us, all over the whole stadium. Some kind of white shreds. I looked at a piece and then picked it up. It was chicken meat.

Bob and Lindsey
'Lindsey, it looks like something's falling from the sky.... I ... I've never seen anything.... What does it look like to you, Lindsey?'

'I, uh, I'm not sure Bob. I know our TV viewers must be as curious as we are. The fans seem rather amused by whatever it is.'

'Play appears to have stopped, sports fans. Uh, there is something falling all over us. It looks like cotton or something, I'm not sure.'

'It's falling straight down, Bob, so I don't think it could be cotton.'

'No, I didn't think it was. I only said it looked like it.... The players are picking it up and they're all shaking their heads. Ron Santo is talking to the third base umpire.... Now he's running into the dugout.... We're trying to get some word from the field on this. Lindsey?' (A long pause during which barely audible whispers are heard.) 'Uh, we'll be back right after this word from our sponsors, sports fans ... *Did you say chick –*'

Aerial Check by Umpires
'Do you see a plane or anything?'

'No, I don't. Do you think a plane's dropping it?'

'What else? You don't think chicken meat would just fall out of the sky, do you? It's some kind of joke.'

'Could be, but I don't see how they could do it. The stuff is coming straight down all over the field, that's the funny part of it. Besides, who'd be crazy enough to fly through that kind of thunderhead?'

'Well, what do you think then?'

'I don't know what to think. I just wish it would stop.'

Condition of the Chicken Meat
Broiled. Edibility unverified for first 26 minutes of fall until sample eaten by W. Montford, New Hyde Park.

Absence of dark meat noted.

Fall Confined to the Actual Area of Shea Stadium
The fall was confined to the actual area of Shea Stadium.[1]

Fortean Events – An Introduction
Fortean events have been known for centuries and have been interpreted in various ways, but never satisfactorily explained. They comprise a wide variety of phenomena.

Devonshire, England, 1837 – a large number of black worms three-quarters of an inch in length fell in a snowstorm.

Vicksburg, Miss., 1894 – a large number of small fish, still alive, fell from the sky.

Sart, France, 1901 – a rain of glue-like substance.

Chico, Calif., 1922 – a shower of warm rocks.

1 Parking lots included. Air vents of several cars clogged.

Worcester, England, 1881 – tons of periwinkle fell in a violent thunderstorm.

Port Isabel, Texas, 1888 – a shower of nails on two successive nights.

Walterboro, S.C., 1886 – a shower of small shot.

Blankenberge, Holland, 1819 – red rain.

Cochin, China, 1887 – a shower of a substance resembling blood, somewhat coagulated.

In Fortean thinking, the universe is perceived as organic, multi-dimensional and teleological. It is also non-metaphysical and largely discoverable by empirical methods. However, the non-acceptance of Fortean hypotheses is due to exclusionism by orthodox science of Fortean events, which cannot be assimilated into the orthodox framework of thought.[2]

Today's Baseball Quiz
Who was the last Philadelphia Phillies player to be the National League's Most Valuable Player?

Two Theological Aspects Considered
A. 'Harvey, this isn't the end of the world, is it?'

'Nah, what's three games out of first place? There's plenty of time to catch up.'

B. The word 'manna' popularly connotes a miraculous 'bread from Heaven.' Biblical manna is believed to be a lichen – *Lecanora esculenta,* perhaps, a plant akin to reindeer moss. Manna that is used for food even today derives from any of a number of plants. In religious literature, it may even include birds.

Destruction of the Stadium Foretold
And Jessie Fleishman, an old embittered Dodger fan, took his Little Leaguers to Flushing to show them the stadium.

2 That such has occurred is explained by Kuhn's thesis, in which scientific research follows a three-stage pattern: 1) a period of largely random and uncoordinated theorizing, unified only by a 'family resemblance' among a general range of phenomena, 2) the establishment of a paradigm or pattern, defining basic beliefs that guide and limit investigation, leading to a dogma, and 3) basic discoveries resulting when research and data fail to reinforce the paradigm. Underlying this thesis is the conviction that the bulk of scientific activity is aimed at establishing the old paradigm and is affected by historical circumstances. Therefore, it is prone to exclusionism. In this frame of thought, Fort's hypotheses may be seen to have passed through all three stages and returned full circle to stage one, with perhaps the most rudimentary formulations of a paradigm.

And Jessie said to them, 'You see this? I swear to you by the spirit of Ebbets Field that this stadium shall be cursed and none shall play in it again.'

And as he sat on the tailgate of his station wagon, his team gathered around him, asking, 'When, Jessie?'

And Jessie answered, 'Don't let anyone fool you. No one can guess the exact day, but there'll be all kinds of rotten stuff happening. It'll serve these hypocrites right.'

The Whiteness of the Chicken Meat
(Told by Sportscaster Ishmael Cosell)

What the chicken meat meant to me is difficult to express. That such material should fall from the sky is pre-eminently appalling, an inexplicable event. Yet, I cannot help but feel that it was the very whiteness of the chicken meat that elicited within my soul a vague horror beyond measure.

Why should this be? Do we not consider whiteness a symbol of virtue, good and beauty? Consider the alabaster sculptures of great artists, the ruins of ancient cities, the raiment of Christ in paintings, or a snow-covered earth at Christmas reflecting the soft light of a full moon.

Yet for all these qualities, there seems to lurk another, diametrically opposed – one of evil. Witness the polar bear, or the white shark or the albatross, a herald of bad luck. In these, the whiteness only serves to intensify the malevolent associations, as if to suggest that these creatures derive their power from a supernatural source.

So it was then with the chicken meat. The whiteness, which contrasted dramatically to the observer's eye with the blackness of the storm clouds from which it fell, seemed to transfix me as well as most of the spectators after a while. Indeed, most had not the presence of mind to put up umbrellas or seek shelter beneath the overhang of the mezzanine. It was as if we were witnessing an act guided by an intelligent but hostile force, against which defense would have been futile.

Effect on Organist Noted

Jane Jarvis tried to amuse the crowd with 'Raindrops Keep Falling On My Head,' but somehow her uneasy spirit was unwilling to make such affectations. Perhaps this was one of the signs in the heavens that presaged the Armageddon. If so, she would face the end at her organ and with it translate the unspeakable bleak

52

mysterious musings of her soul into music. So it was that 47,000 people allowed chicken meat to rain upon their heads as they listened to Franck's *Fantaisie in A Major.*

Meanwhile, In the TV Booth

'Folks, we're talking to Mr. Elmer Yarg, an old-time colleague of Bob and myself, during this, uh, delay ... Elmer, remember those days in the International League?'

'What?'

'I said, remember those days in the International League?'

Elmer stared at the white dots on Lindsey's tie, which seemed to quiver like snowflakes against a streetlight. 'I, uh ... don't remember off hand,' was his monotone response.

Mrs. Fenwick from Bayside's Irritation

'I've had enough of this, Charlie. Let's go home.'

'The game hasn't been called off yet, Marion. Maybe this'll stop and they'll finish.'

'I don't care. I'm worried about Mother. She's all by herself.'

'What's to worry? She'll be okay.'

'I don't care. Let's go.'

Charlie sat quietly. There's nothing to worry about. They could be happy right here. Free food falling out of the sky, plenty of beer vendors, even bathrooms. Actually, they could stay forever or until the end of the season, whichever came first.

'Are you coming or am I going to go home by myself?'

'Marion ... please,' said Charlie with exaggerated calmness. 'There is ... nothing ... to worry about.'

'Are you crazy? Look at this! You call this normal?'

'No, I ...'

'It's not good, whatever it is, and we'd better get back home. For the last time, will you get up?'

Her husband did not answer but sat pensively even as a piece of chicken fell on his head. 'Then I'm leaving alone.' She gathered her windbreaker and handbag in a flurry of motion and suddenly stopped.

Her husband looked at her. 'I thought you were going.'

'I.... I can't move! I'm trying to move but I can't.'

Charlie turned his eyes back to the field, where the tarpaulin had been laid down for lack of any better strategy. 'Of course not,' he said. 'Nobody can. Nobody wants to leave.'

'What do you mean, nobody wants to leave?' she said, alarmed.

'Subconsciously, we want to stay.'

'What?'

'The collective subconscious. We're all part of it, so we can't leave because it doesn't want us to leave.'

'Why not?'

Charlie paused for a moment. 'I'm not sure.... It's ... it's ... like part of us is controlling all the other parts. I don't know.'

'Charlie, we'll starve!'

He smiled as a mathematician might at the logic of a theorem. 'Hold out your hands.'

Radio Bulletin

'And now, this late word.... At Shea Stadium, the Mets baseball game with the Cubs has been delayed by – *get this, folks* – a *shower of chicken meat.* (Laughter in background.) Several eye-witness reports of the phenomenon were just phoned in to us by sports writers at the scene. (More laughter.) The chicken meat has been falling in white shreds of uniform size and in a cooked condition. There have been severe thunderstorms scattered about the metropolitan area, but only at the stadium has the chicken meat been falling. The Police Dept. has stated there is no emergency and no cause for alarm, but neither they nor the weather bureau have any explanation for these *fowl* goings-on. (High-pitched outburst of laughter.)

'Now a word from Farrago Premium Margarine ...'
(Allegro moderato)
'Far-ra-go
Far-ra-go
Farrago Premi-yum-yum-yum,
It's so good in your tummy-tum-tum,
It's good on bread, especially toast,
In recipes it is the most
Delicious and nutritious, too,
Farrago is the one for you.
It's good when you're up,
It's good when you're down,
It will make you smile, but never frown,
So when you shop, don't mess around,
Get the one that's world renowned –

Far-ra-go
Far-ra-go
Farrago Premi-yummmm.'

Soliloquy of a Hot Dog Vendor

I remember times that I was dreaming and I could watch myself like from some detached vantage point, like watching an old movie on TV on a channel with bad reception. I had that same feeling watching the chicken fall, covering the field like a white carpet, as if God were throwing up. Most everything was quiet like in a church, except for a few babies crying. And the stuff just kept dropping in whooshes and plops. I sat down in an aisle and leaned my head on the hot dog box and closed my eyes. But it was like I had X-ray eyes and could still see everything. Strange things popped into my mind, like bodies rising from graves and a ticket seller dying as punishment for not selling out his section. Maybe other planets were trying to communicate and why didn't they consider something like this in the comic books. I knew I would never sell another hot dog and some one else would have to replace me. The chicken meat would crush flower beds and suffocate babies left outside in their carriages, and ambulances on the way to the hospital would skid and crash. I was glad it was happening, I really was. The whole world was going to change, like people must have thought when they went to see a weeping madonna or when those guys landed on the moon. All around the world people's souls would leave their bodies and they could stop eating or drinking or worrying about being shot. They should bring all the criminals here and let them see this. That would be something.

Progression Along a Vertical Vector

One inch, then two inches. A foot. The level of the meat rose higher. One row after another was lost from view. Mercifully, those in the seats fell into a deep trance before being asphyxiated. The entire lower deck was lost in one hour and twenty minutes. The mezzanine followed within another hour as the shower accelerated. The loge and upper deck seemed oblivious. Even Jane Jarvis went on playing soulful works by dead geniuses and melodies that entered her head from some unknown source. The stadium's face was white and strange-smelling in the breeze. The scores on the scoreboard were submerged one by one and starting pitchers and their relievers in both leagues fell quietly dead on fields all around the country. An Air Force helicopter clattered loudly above the stadium for a minute, then flew away. Ringing phones in the press box went unanswered and finally stopped. All was quiet as death save for the plopping of the chicken meat and the flapping of the flag, flicking north, then east, then northeast, barely five feet above the level of the tide when the shower finally ceased.

Answer to Baseball Quiz
Jim Konstanty – 1950.

West Quaco

I was in the company of my old friend Strauss, a Viennese engineer, whom I had not seen for many years. I had proposed to him that we take a motor trip across the eastern part of the country – something I had wanted to do for a long time – and enjoy ourselves for three weeks before he set to work overseeing the refitting of the plant his company had just purchased here. Accordingly, Strauss had arranged to take his vacation leave early, and I, for my part, had just delivered a new manuscript to my publisher and cleared my desk of all other obligations.

Our plan was to rent a car and drive to the east coast by one route and back by another. Everything went well for two weeks. The weather was fine, the countryside was at its most beautiful, we ate well, we slept well, and I, for one, was having the best vacation of my life.

It was on the way back that our trip took an unexpected turn. Foolishly, I had allowed us to run low on gas on a stretch of road that had no service stations, and our map indicated we had a fair way to go until the next town. Suddenly, Strauss said, 'Turn there,' as we came upon a sign with fading letters that read 'West Quaco,' with an arrow pointing to the right. Underneath, the word 'gas' had been nailed on crookedly. Strauss checked the map. 'It's not on the map.'

'Probably too small,' I said.

I turned onto the narrow road, which we followed for five or six kilometers until we reached a small town. It seemed very quiet, almost deserted. The first thing that caught our attention was a gleaming red Texaco sign on a large pole beside a partially-built station. There was a large hole in the ground with a tank in it and a heap of dirt beside it. New pumps stood on their concrete islands with their insides exposed.

As we parked the car and got out, a boy in a clean Texaco uniform came out to meet us. The name 'Herman' was stitched on his uniform. 'You want a gas, sir?' he asked.

'Do you have gas?' asked Strauss.

'A gas?' asked Herman.

'*Gas,*' said Strauss emphatically. 'We'd like some gas if you have any.'

I wondered whether the boy was retarded, for he seemed to gaze at Strauss uncomprehendingly. 'You want a gas, right?'

'Not *a* gas,' said Strauss, slightly annoyed. '*Gas. Gasoline. We want gasoline.*'

'Yes, sir, a gasoline.'

'Okay, have it your way. Do you have any?'

The boy seemed to become slightly nervous. 'M-m-m-maybe in a little while. The delivery truck is coming.'

Strauss frowned as he gave the station a once-over. 'Is there another gas station anywhere around here?'

'No, sir, nowhere.'

Strauss considered the situation. I decided to let him figure it out for us since his was the scientific mind, not mine. 'Where's your boss?'

'Across the street,' Herman said, pointing with a hand that had too many fingers, it seemed to me. 'Ray's Sporting Goods.'

'Is that your boss – Ray?'

'Yes, speak to Ray.'

'Okay to leave the car here?'

'Yes, sir. If you will let me have the keys, I will take it out back and give it a nice wash. No charge.' He smiled.

Strauss handed him the keys. 'Okay. Thanks.'

We headed across the street to Ray's. The store looked pretty shabby from the outside. Inside, it looked even worse. The entire store was a mess. What's more, it seemed to contain only three kinds of merchandise – skis, golf balls, and athletic socks. Oh, yes, there was one other thing – a bowling ball, set like some valuable necklace on a blue velvet pillow in the display case beside the cash register. It had a sign on it: 'My Championship Ball – Not For Sale.' After these words the words 'AT ANY PRICE!!' had been added as an angry afterthought. Next to the ball was a framed picture. It showed a smiling man receiving a trophy. The caption typed on an index card under the photo said: 'Ray Bluth, St. Louis, Mo. – Leading PBA Average 1964 – 210.512.'

An old man was holding a pair of socks in a corner of the store. He was absolutely rigid as he examined them up close, as if looking at the individual threads of the fabric. There was something strange about his head: the back of it seemed virtually as flat as a board.

Ray, a middle-aged man, came out from behind the filthy, cluttered counter. 'Yes, can I help you?'

'We wanted some gas,' said Strauss. 'We're stuck, I'm afraid. We're down to practically nothing.'

Ray sighed genially, his hands in his pockets. 'We will have gas – eventually.'

At this point I piped in, 'The sign on the main highway said "gas."'

'Yes,' said Ray, 'but it didn't say when.' He smiled apologetically. 'Are you fellows in a hurry?'

'No, not really,' said Strauss. 'But how long will we have to wait?'

'A couple of hours maybe.'

Strauss looked at me, and I gave him a look that said, 'What can you do?' I cast a sideways glance at the old man. He was still engrossed with the pair of socks.

'Tell you what,' said Ray. 'Why don't I take you fellows over to the cafe and treat you to a coffee and a bite to eat? I don't get a chance to speak to outsiders much. Not that I miss the outside.'

'You're not from around here?' asked Strauss.

'No, from St. Louis.' He started herding us toward the door.

'What about your customer?' I asked.

'He's not a customer. He lives here, sort of.'

As we exited I gave the old man another look. He was drooling on the socks.

Outside, I saw that our car had already disappeared. A brief feeling of foreboding hit me, but I dismissed it.

Strauss remarked to Ray, 'You don't seem to be doing much business.'

'*Much* business? Hell, I don't do *any* practically.'

'Then why do you stay here?'

At this, Ray's expression became sadly intense. 'There are things in life that are more important than money. There's *appreciation,* for instance. These people appreciate my championship form.' And so saying, he made a motion with an imaginary bowling ball to demonstrate it, ending with a triumphant little punch to indicate a perfect strike.

We walked down the middle of the main street. The town consisted of this main street plus a few short alleys or side-streets. There were perhaps a few dozen run-down buildings in all. The town seemed abnormally quiet. Strauss and I had passed through scores of small towns, yet this one struck me as somehow different, in a way that was hard to put my finger on. Aside from the new Texaco station, it seemed so unconnected to the rest of the world. I think it was the absence of traffic that gave me this feeling. A lady passed us whose nose appeared to be way off center. She was carrying what appeared to be a dead cat. She and Ray exchanged nods of recognition.

On the side of a building I saw a sign: *'Hezekiah Says: Persistence of obsession to dominate is as instinctive as a calf looking for its dam to suckle.'* I was about to ask our host the meaning of this when he began to speak again, this time with a lump in his throat. I thought he was holding back tears. 'You see, I'm washed up in bowling. Washed up. Completely. All because of a little misunderstanding.' He paused, perhaps unsure of whether to take us into his confidence. 'I was out for a walk late one night and somebody in a gorilla suit beat me up and stole my pants. I was arrested for indecent exposure. Of course, nobody believed me.' He looked at us to gauge our reactions. I tried to look sympathetic. Strauss seemed mildly amused. 'You believe me, don't you?'

'Of course,' said Strauss.

'And afterwards, well ...' A long pause. 'My game went all to hell. I couldn't concentrate.'

'I understand,' said Strauss. 'By the way, were you convicted, if you don't mind my asking?'

'No, the charge was dropped for insufficient evidence. But my reputation was still ruined. And then ...' He sighed. 'I ended up here, pretty much by chance. It's a long story, not worth going into. Anyway, I bought the store to have something to do. Got it for next to nothing. Same with the gas station. Just got that recently.'

The cafe he took us to was called The Skinned Woman Cafe, a name that struck me as macabre. Inside, the place was gloomy and dirty. Four or five patrons sat in booths or at the counter. Strauss nudged me. 'Look at that.' I looked and beheld the very thing that had given the cafe its name. Reader, believe me when I tell you that displayed prominently on the wall was the complete skin of a white adult woman. The sight of it sent a shudder through me. Strauss, undaunted, stepped right up to it to get a good look. My friend had always had a keen scientific curiosity about anything unusual.

'That's the skinned woman,' Ray explained to me matter-of-factly, leading me to a booth. 'Or rather, it's the skinned woman's skin. Where the skinned woman herself is, I don't know.'

The proprietor came over and set paper place mats and glasses of water before us. I was fascinated by the man's face. His eyes were abnormally far apart, and one ear was far larger than the other. 'Howdy,' he said.

'Hello,' I answered. 'Set a place for my friend too,' I said, indicating Strauss. I looked around at the other patrons. They all seemed physically abnormal. One man looked as though a wedge-shaped object had been imbedded in his skull. He appeared to be eating a piece of raw liver. A lady of indeterminate age had a sort of hairy, bulbous growth under her neck. A boy reading a comic book had hideous eruptions or sores on one arm. Our host, Ray, was quite normal. But then, like us, he came from the 'outside.'

Strauss sat down beside me. 'Extraordinary,' he said to me. Then he asked the proprietor, 'Where on earth did you get that skin?'

'She was here before I was,' the man replied. 'My grandfather got her from an old gun collector in nineteen-fourteen, and he kept her in his shop as a conversation piece. He was a taxidermist. Then my father inherited her and put her here in the cafe when he opened it.' He handed us a menu. 'She's a beauty, ain't she?'

'Yes,' agreed Strauss.

'Who was she?' I asked kiddingly.

'I don't see that that's any of *your* business,' he said.

I looked at my placemat. It contained these words: '*Hezekiah Says: If we want protection from the oceans of evil storms, we must instigate the cultivation and growth of good trees.*'

Ray ordered pie and coffee for the three of us. It was brought to us by a waitress who had incredibly huge, sharp teeth. I excused myself to go to the toilet. Inadvertently, I barged in on the proprietor, who was peeing into a tin cup. I said excuse me and backed out. I waited. He came out, wiping his lips with the back of his hand. I reentered and saw the tin cup on a shelf beside the sink. It smelled of urine. My feeling of foreboding came back. I didn't like this West Quaco, and the sooner we got out the better.

I returned to the table, unable to eat my pie. I gave it to Strauss. I refused to drink the coffee and would only sip a bit of water after discreetly smelling it.

Ray did indeed treat us. As he was paying the cheque, I pulled Strauss aside and said to him, 'The owner drinks his own urine. I saw him.'

'You don't say!'

'And have you noticed these people? They're all deformed.'

'Mmm.'

'I want to get out of this place now. Before dark.' It was late afternoon.

Strauss reminded Ray politely of our need for gas. Ray replied, 'The truck's coming. And anyway, if need be, we can put you up for the night.' Alarm bells went off in my head.

Strauss forced a smile. 'Fine. Well, while we're waiting, what else is there to see in this town?'

'I'll take you to see our shrine, if you like.'

'A shrine! Splendid!' Strauss had a great interest in church architecture.

We stepped out into the street. I could have sworn a man with three arms passed us, but I didn't have the courage to turn around for a second look. Strauss was smiling. A sign in a window said, *Hezekiah Says: In the old days men could fly by singing a song and striking a plate.'*

The shrine Ray spoke of did indeed look like a church, albeit one of modest size. Over the door was the name 'The Shrine of Mussolini's Shorts.'

'I have to warn you about the Cardinal,' said Ray. 'He's, well, let's say a bit temperamental. He can't stand skeptics or intellectuals, so don't disagree with him or act too smart. Um ... I'll tell you, he *can* be violent at times, but otherwise he's a regular guy.'

Ray ushered us inside, where we found a ceremony taking place. The Cardinal, dressed in a beautiful scarlet robe and wearing a splendid mitre, had his back to us and was kneeling before an altar with a glass case containing an item of underwear. A ring of candles surrounded the altar. Eight or ten parishioners knelt in their pews. The wall ahead of us was dominated by a huge portrait of Mussolini in military uniform. Lugubrious organ music was coming in faintly from somewhere. The Cardinal was saying, 'Oh, Benito Mussolini, Our Light of Lights, Our Hope of Hopes, you founded the Italian Fascist Party to restore the Glory that was Rome. After your election to Parliament in nineteen-twenty-one, you attracted ever-increasing rightist support, culminating in your March on Rome in October of nineteen-twenty-two and the subsequent resignation of the government ...'

Ray whispered to me, 'This brings tears to my eyes.' Indeed, several of the other parishioners seemed to be crying. Ray led us into a pew and motioned to us to kneel.

'... King Victor Emmanuel the Third called upon you, Il Duce, to form a cabinet. You made Italy a corporate state. You made the trains and rivers run on time. You signed the Lateran Treaty in nineteen-twenty-nine, resolving the old conflicts with the Church caused by the annexation of the Papal States in eighteen-seventy, and thus enjoyed the Church's increased support. You invaded Ethiopia in nineteen-thirty-five. Oh, what a glorious moment it was! You annexed Albania in nineteen-thirty-nine and formed a military alliance with Nazi Germany. But then, after the Allies landed in Italy in nineteen-forty-three, you were forced to resign ...' Ray was weeping into his hanky. '... And Marshal Badoglio sued for peace. You were rescued by the Germans and later attempted to regain power, but it was too late. Germany fell, and you were shot while trying to escape to Switzerland. Now we have only your shorts to remember you by, this holiest of holy garments. Through your shorts you are still with us, Benito, inspiring us upward into Infinite Glory. Amen.' He stood up and faced his parishioners. 'Go now in peace, my children.' The organ music was suddenly replaced by a lively polka. (The significance of this escapes me to this day.)

We stood up. Ray led us forward through the exiting parishioners and introduced us to His Eminence, Cardinal Ratnozo, who seemed delighted to have visitors from the outside. He was also flattered by our interest and encouraged us to look at Mussolini's shorts up close. I could see that they were white boxer-type shorts and that they bore the monogram 'B.M.' I was about to ask a question, but I remembered Ray's warning. Strauss, however, boldly asked the Cardinal, 'Your Eminence, what possible spiritual significance can Mussolini's underwear have?'

Cardinal Ratnozo gave him a stern look. 'This is a matter of faith. I can see that you have had your faith poisoned by too much education. Without faith we are nothing. We must believe and accept. This is also a matter of local tradition.'

Strauss said he understood and hoped His Eminence would forgive him. The latter smiled. A possible altercation had been averted. 'Perhaps you would like to see faith at work. There is a sick man I must see. His suffering is great. I must go to comfort him.'

Naturally, Strauss was all too eager to go along. As we walked a few paces behind Ray and the Cardinal, I said to him in a low voice, 'This place scares me. I want to get out.'

'Not just yet. It's just getting interesting. I want to see everything.'

63

Outside, I spied yet another of Hezekiah's sayings, painted on the side of a junked car: *'Hezekiah Says: Sometimes the best way out of a wilderness is on a cow.'*

I ventured to ask His Eminence, 'Who is this Hezekiah anyway?'

'A great and mysterious man. He lives right here in town.'

'I think I'd like to pay him a visit just for the hell of it.'

'NO!' The Cardinal stopped and glared at me. 'It is not permitted for outsiders to meet Hezekiah! This is a great sin! Do not speak of it again!'

'Gee, I'm sorry.'

He gave me a faint smile to reassure me. We continued walking. He touched the back of his neck. 'Boy, my hair's getting good in the back.' And then, dear reader, he lifted his mitre, and I saw to my shock that his head was cone-shaped like the mitre itself! He felt his hair up and down the back of his head, then put his mitre back on. I looked up at Strauss. He looked positively thrilled.

Ray left us at this point, saying he had to get back to his store and 'rub the old man's feet.' What he meant by that, I don't know. He said he hoped to see us later and went off in the other direction, making bowling motions down the middle of the street.

I expected Cardinal Ratnozo to lead us to a hospital, but I should not have been surprised to learn there was no hospital in a town as small as West Quaco. We were led instead into the basement of a nondescript vacant building, where a room had been fitted out as a sort of ward. 'Stay here. It is not permitted for you to enter the Room of Salvation,' he said at the threshold.

Reader, I am a sensitive man, and it pains me to set down in writing the scene that took place. To begin with, the suffering man's bed was partly surrounded by a screen; thus my friend and I could not actually see him. But his groans of agony convinced me that he was in such a terrible condition that I could not likely have stood the sight of him. Most assuredly, he was gasping his last breaths. Several old ladies in white (they may have been nuns, but I'm not sure) crowded around the bed. They would administer dressings which left my view in a clean white condition and, after a short interval, came into sight again as sopping red cloths. A pile of these bloody dressings was building in a basin on the floor.

The Cardinal, his back to us, was leaning over the man, and it seemed to me that he took some sort of implement from inside his robe. Immediately as the Cardinal leaned over the man, a heart-rending scream filled the air.

'AAAGGHHHH! OOOHH! EEEGGHH!'

'There now, Brother, be calm.'

'AAAGGHHH! NO! NO! STOP! UNNGGHH!'

'Hush, Brother, you are offending the Lord.'

'NO! NO! OW! OW! UNNGH!'

I gripped Strauss's arm. 'We have to do something. He's killing him.'

'No, we can't interfere,' he replied, his brow creased with tension.

'NO! AAAGH! AAGH! OW! OW!'

'Stop screaming, Brother. Don't you know you are going to Heaven?'

'UUNNNGH! UNGH! HELP! OH, HELP!'

'Yes, Brother, Heaven. How lucky you are. I wish I could be in your place.'

A yelp escaped the man's lips that seemed like that of a castrated horse.

'How I envy you your pain, Brother. Your heavenly reward awaits.'

We heard a faint groan and then nothing. Had the man died, or had he merely passed out? My face was wet with tears. I felt nauseous.

The Cardinal wiped his hands first on a cloth towel. Then one of the women handed him a little foil packet. The logo on the outside caught my eye: it was a pre-moistened towelette from Kentucky Fried Chicken! The Cardinal unfolded the wet paper towel and cleaned his bloody hands thoroughly.

I said to Strauss in a low voice, 'This is the last straw. We have to get out of here.'

'All right, all right.'

'Promise me. Don't let the sun go down on us in this town.'

'We have to see about the car.'

'I have a feeling they're going to keep us here.'

'Don't be silly. Your imagination's running away with you.'

I put my faith at last in Strauss's sang-froid. Had I been with anyone else, I would have been beside myself with fear.

Cardinal Ratnozo came out of the room, beaming with satisfaction.

'Is he dead?' I asked.

'Almost, thank God. His body cannot be saved, but his soul can.' He sniffed his fingers. 'Ahhh ... but I sure hate it when they scream like that, the bloody cowards.'

At this, a look of outrage crossed Strauss's face, but he held himself back.

I was glad to get out of that torture chamber and back onto the street. A moment after we stepped outdoors, a bee whizzed past Ratnozo's face. 'OH, NO! HELP! GET IT AWAY FROM ME!' He fell to the ground, terror-stricken. The bee buzzed around him a few times and then flew away. He was shaking. 'God, a bee, there's nothing worse!' We helped him up and brushed the dirt off his robe. Oddly, his mitre had remained firmly in place. After a few deep breaths to regain his composure, he was soon smiling again. 'What do you say we go hoist a few?'

'I beg your pardon?' asked Strauss.

'He means, let's have a few drinks,' I explained.

'Good idea!' said Strauss. I couldn't tell whether he really wanted to drink or whether he merely wanted an opportunity to observe Cardinal Ratnozo further. Probably both.

'We need gas for our car,' I blurted out. 'Have you got any?'

His Eminence frowned at me. 'Brother, where is your faith?'

He took us to his house, a large dilapidated structure whose grounds were choked with weeds. A housekeeper opened the door. She was a hunchbacked dwarf whom the Cardinal addressed as 'my dear Carlotta.' We were seated in the living room, where we found ourselves surrounded by ancient devices of torture, including a rack, an Iron Maiden, a table of some sort equipped with straps and sharp metal spikes, and a framework of wooden beams with several sets of manacles hanging over them. There were stacks of magazines all over the place that appeared to deal with sadism.

The Cardinal's 'dear Carlotta' brought us some cold beer − *Miller High Life,* no less.

'Pretty grim place you have here,' I said.

'One might see it that way,' the Cardinal replied.

A second look at the table of torture revealed what I took to be blood stains. 'I don't suppose you actually still use these devices?'

'Oh, no, of course not.' He chuckled. 'This is a sort of museum. But my assistant and I do conduct various researches, as it happens.'

'Your assistant?'

'Yes. He has a laboratory in the basement. Perhaps you'd like to meet him.'

'Yes!' said Strauss at once.

'Good. Let's peek in on him. His name is Innocent, and he was once the head of a vice squad in a big city many years ago.'

'A police officer? How interesting!' said Strauss.

'What did you say his name was?' I asked.

'Innocent, like that of fourteen of the Popes.'

'Thirteen,' corrected Strauss.

The Cardinal gave him a brief look of hostility, then smiled again. 'Of course, I meant thirteen.' He opened the basement door and led us down the stairs.

'Harrr! Harrr! Harrr!' we heard a voice say. Innocent was naked, sitting on a stool by a workbench, looking into a microscope. He made a note on a pad. 'Another sodomist! Good!'

I expected to see some physical abnormality, but then I remembered that he was not a native-born West Quaconian. He was, however, a singularly ugly man. As we approached him, I saw that he had a prodigious erection, which he made not the slightest effort to hide.

'Innocent,' said the Cardinal, 'two visitors from the outside would like to know what you're working on.'

'Ants!' he said, turning a fierce face toward us. His eyes were wide and maniacal.

'Ants?' I asked. 'Why ants?'

Innocent explained: 'All my life I have been interested in all forms of sexual degeneracy and perversion. Many years ago I came to the conclusion that it was an innate biological trait, common not only to Man but to all animal life. I asked myself, "What is the true source of these sins? When did they begin?" This led me to pursue Sin throughout the animal kingdom, starting with Man and working backward to more primitive forms of life. And now ...' He paused, sitting up straight with a triumphant look. '... I believe I have discovered the true source of Sin! I call them... *the Pervert Ants!*'

I could see several ants on the microscope slide. He beckoned me to look for myself. As I put my eye to the eyepiece, he said, 'Here is the full panorama of sexual deviancy – oral sex, sodomy, sadism, masochism, fetishism, homosexuality, bestiality, troilism, urolagnia, coprolagnia, rape, sexual murder, and even indecent exposure!' I couldn't see anything except magnified ants.

'May I see?' asked Strauss.

I made room for him. He looked carefully for a full minute while Innocent prattled on: 'The Pervert Ants are the true source of Original Sin, which means that Man is not responsible. So until God punishes the ants, Man is free to act as he pleases – sex-wise, at least.' He went on in this vein while walking around in a circle excitedly, his erection dangling like a billy club. Then he broke out into a little song:

> 'Oh, my Pervert Ants,
> Pervert, Pervert, Pervert Ants,
> Me and my Pervert Ants,
> Cocka wocka focka.'

'Astonishing. Truly astonishing,' said Strauss at last. I knew he hadn't seen anything either. Innocent and the Cardinal looked very pleased.

We begged leave of our host at this point. Strauss said we had to go to the gas station to see about our car. The Cardinal bade us farewell and presented us with an autographed copy of his pamphlet, *The Significance of Mussolini's Shorts for Human Salvation*. Before the door closed behind us, we heard his dear Carlotta say to him, 'The donkey is ready, Sire.'

As we hastened back to the other end of town, I said to Strauss 'Maybe the gas truck has arrived. Then we can fill up and get out of here.'

'There's no gas truck coming. There can't possibly be.'

'Why not?'

'Because that station isn't ready to pump gas. I could tell in an instant.'

'Hell, why didn't you tell me this right away?'

'Their little lie aroused my curiosity. Then that Ray fellow and his store. Very odd, very odd. I wanted to scout around, but if I'd told you, you'd have gotten scared.'

'I'm scared now. We're prisoners, don't you see? God, what'll we do?'

'Don't panic. I'll get us out of here. It's time to be a little more aggressive, that's all.'

The look of determination on his face gave me hope. I saw that the sun was getting low. If we were not out of there before dark, who knew what might happen to us?

I was hoping to see our car in front of the gas station, but it wasn't there. And a quick look showed us that it wasn't out back either. Herman, the attendant, saw us. He looked frightened. He stepped out of the office with a small basket of fruit in his hand. 'I have a fruits for you, sir,' he said.

'Never mind that!' Strauss growled. 'We want our car now, and we want gas too!'

'Y-y-your c-c-car?'

'We want our car now! Or else!'

The terrified boy dropped the basket of fruit and seemed to go into a kind of fit. His head rotated back and forth like a radar antenna. *'Brrrp brrrp brrrp ... potato warning,'* he said in a robot-like voice. *'Brrrp brrrp brrrp ... potato warning ... brrrp brrrp brrrp ... potato warning ... brrrp brrrp brrrp ... potato warning ...'*

'Enough of this bullshit,' said Strauss to me. 'Let's go to the sheriff's office.'

We had noticed a building marked 'Sheriff' on our way back. We retraced our steps quickly and went in the front door. We found ourselves in a sort of anteroom or vestibule containing a coat rack (nothing on it), a little table with a dead plant in a pot, and a switchboard that was literally covered with dust and cobwebs. It looked as though someone had taken a dozen whacks at it with an axe. We opened the next door and saw a man sitting behind a huge wooden desk, writing or doodling on a pad. The room seemed like a combination office and living quarters, with file cabinets and shelves alternating with chests, wardrobes, and a bed. Clothes were scattered everywhere.

The sheriff was a huge hulk of a man with a shock of white hair that stuck out all over. Behind him in a large cage suspended from the ceiling were two monkeys. 'Yes?' he said.

'Are you the sheriff?' asked Strauss.

'Yes, I'm Sheriff Filbert. Forgive me for not rising. I have a medical condition that is unpleasant to look at. It also hampers my mobility. Please sit down.' He indicated two chairs before his desk. We sat down. The monkeys made little chattering noises and seemed to smile at us.

'Your badge says "Fireman,"' Strauss observed.

'I can be a fireman if I want to be,' said Sheriff Filbert rather defensively. 'I'm also known as the Super Detective. In Spanish, that would be El Super Detectivo, although nobody around here speaks Spanish.'

Good grief, I thought.

'Indeed,' said Strauss. 'Well, if you're a super detective, you ought to be able to help us. It seems we arrived almost out of gas and left our car – '

'Hold it, hold it,' said the sheriff, picking up a fresh legal-size pad and a purple crayon. 'We must start at the very beginning. I must know who you are, where you come from, all the relevant background.'

'But really —'

'No but's. We do things by the book around here. If there is a mystery to be solved, it will require the highest faculties of the rational mind and all available data.' The monkeys got more excited and jumped from perch to perch in their cage.

Strauss gave the sheriff a full chronological report of our situation, beginning with his arrival in the country for the purpose of supervising the refitting of his company's new plant. It was marvellous to listen to the clarity and conciseness with which he expressed himself, sparing no detail, yet never repeating himself. The sheriff scribbled furiously with his purple crayon, but it seemed to me that he was just making meaningless marks on paper. At one point, when Strauss paused to allow the sheriff to catch up to him, I asked 'What kind of writing is that?'

'It's shorthand,' replied the sheriff with a hint of anger. At that moment the monkeys began making hissing noises and glaring at me. 'It's called Filbert Shorthand. I invented it myself,' he added, his tone calm again. The monkeys became calm again too.

'Oh, I see. By the way, what kind of monkeys are those?'

'They're indicator monkeys. They help put you in touch with your inner feelings. They help you to know yourself.' Strauss and I exchanged significant looks.

Strauss continued his narrative, this time more slowly, as if studying each individual mark made by the sheriff in response to his words. I was now convinced the marks were meaningless. Strauss explained about our car and then briefly recounted all that had happened to us in town.

'Okay, now let me see if I have this all right,' the sheriff said, flipping back to the first page. 'Ahem... *The double standard system in everyone's mind are old ideology development gained in Moses' days that have never been outgrown into the true meaning of Our Lord's knowledge —*'

'I never said that,' said Strauss.

'Quiet! Let me finish!' the sheriff snapped, as the monkeys jabbered and hooted angrily, jumping about so that the cage swung back and forth. '*Today mankind's mind is becoming destroyed through self-indignation that flounders the minds with emotional disabilities, to react their anxieties of insecurities, to be spoken for mistaken knowledge, in open communications to one another, to form poor communication blocks to one another —*'

'This is ridiculous!' I protested.

'Don't interrupt!' the sheriff said, flipping the page, as the monkeys bared their teeth and hissed at us ferociously. *'Our Lord unlocked the strait method of using one's mind whole in true self-directed thinking, right through the motor system controlled in the genes and chromosomes, which is the producing machine, when mankind learns to think accurately –'*

Strauss stood up and said to me, 'This man is insane. Let's get out of here.' We got up and started to leave.

'... Indignation is the floundering system – STOP! I'M NOT FINISHED!' He rose from his seat, and we saw that he was naked below the waist and that he possessed a hard scrotal tumor the size of a basketball. *'TO KEEP THE MIND IN AN IMBALANCE SYSTEM OF THOUGHTS THAT CAUSES ANYONE TO PRESSURE THEIR EMOTIONAL FEELINGS ...'*

We got out of there as fast as we could, with the sheriff's voice mingling with the wild hooting of the monkeys and the desperate swinging of their cage.

'What do we do now?' I asked.

'Let's go back and see Ray. He's the least crazy of any of them. He may be our last hope.'

We headed back to Ray's store. As we walked in, a sudden inspiration hit me. 'Ray,' I said, 'I think you're the best damn bowler who ever lived! Would you show us your championship form again?'

His face lit up. 'Why ... why sure!' And he picked up an imaginary ball and went through his motion.

'Wonderful! Wonderful!' exclaimed Strauss, following my cue. 'If only my friends in Vienna could see such beauty!'

'Oh, my! Oh, my!' said Ray, close to tears.

'Say, Ray,' I went on, 'could you settle a bet for us? Strauss says you have six sanctioned three-hundred games to your credit, and I say seven. Which is it?'

'I have twelve!'

'Twelve! Wow!' I said.

I knew that one of us had to broach the crucial question. I decided to. 'Ray, look, we want to go home. Can you get us our car back with a little gas, whatever you can scrape up?'

'Heh, heh, well ...' He looked down at his shoes. I felt an awful moment of tension until he looked up at us and smiled. 'Well, sure, sure, I reckon we can work something out. But you've got to be prepared to do us a little favor.'

'Okay, you name it.'

71

'Let's go over to the general store,' he said.

Ray took us down the street to the general store. Underneath an old Coke logo, a sign had been hung: 'Hezekiah Says: The surge of parrot psychology comes on strong, like a persistent potato.'

After all that had happened, I was not the least surprised to see that the storekeeper, named Clem, had a six-inch horn projecting out of his forehead that curved down in front of his nose. Ray introduced us and then went into the back room with Clem for a little conference while we waited.

'We should buy some groceries to take with us on the road,' I said.

'Hmm. I wonder,' said Strauss, looking around.

Looking more closely, I saw the most improbable sorts of products. Almost an entire wall was filled with row after row of packages of a kind of sausage. I picked one up. It was called *Beefalooka*. The slogan on the package said, *'The beef jerky Joe Palooka would eat if he were a real person.'* It looked extremely dry. The expiry date on the package had passed more than two years before.

My attention was also caught by a hideous black breakfast cereal called *Coalies*, a peculiar rubber implement called *Popeil's Pocket Woman*, *Bulgarian Revenge Cologne*, *City Slicker Dehydrated Squid Soup*, *Valley of Despair Cat Food*, *Redundant Power Moose Deodorant*, *President Millard Fillmore Pig Brain Jelly*, *Armageddon Edible Suspenders*, *Angry Buttocks Laxative*, something called *Mixed Molluscs* in an cellophane bag, *Borx Horse Mouthwash*, *Zorro Condoms*, *Morose Earwig Tuna*, *Old Turkish Pajamas Chewing Tobacco*, *Witch Whey*, *Pakistan Power Sponges*, and a barrel of grey granules without any sort of label. I decided I could go hungry for another couple of hours.

'Look at this,' said Strauss, handing me a pack of trading cards like the ones kids collect. There was a box of them on the counter. The pop-up display board read: '*MICRO-COON – The Three-Inch-Tall Negro Who Can Fly and Solve World Problems.*' The packs cost twenty-five cents apiece.

'I can't resist,' I said to Strauss as I put a quarter on the counter. I opened the pack and found a nice pink square of bubble gum, which I popped in my mouth. It was watermelon-flavored.

There were five *Micro-Coon* cards in the pack. The first one was captioned: *'Micro-Coon brings Menachem Begin and Yasser Arafat together.'* The cartoon showed Begin and Arafat shaking hands and clapping each other on the back as Micro-Coon hovered above them. In the background, on the desert, bearded sheiks and Orthodox rabbis were cheering and dancing with each other. On the back of the card it said: '*Card no. 25 – Collect the Whole Set of 100! Since the creation of the Jewish state of Israel in 1948, many Arabs have fought for the return of the ancient land of Palestine. The Palestine Liberation Organization (PLO) and its leader, Yasser Arafat, were the sworn enemies of Israel and its leader, Menachem Begin. But one day Micro-Coon went to each of them and spoke to them of love, friendship, and peace. The boyish twinkle in his eye softened the hearts of these hard-liners. The next day he brought them together over lunch, where they talked over their differences and became friends. Copyright 1980, Tasteful Gum Company, Hicksville, New York.*'

The other cards were captioned '*Micro-Coon reasons with a hijacker,*' '*Micro-Coon relieves drought victims in Chad,*' '*Micro-Coon brings about nuclear disarmament,*' and '*Micro-Coon addresses the International Conference on the Ozone Layer.*'

My reading was interrupted by the return of Ray. 'Okay, fellows, listen, here's the deal. You get your car and some gas, but you have to take Clem's daughter off his hands.'

'What do you mean?' I asked.

'Clem's daughter is, how shall I put it, *abnormal*. He'd like you to take her to a hospital in the big city and get her fixed up. Then you can send her back. We'll pay the bills, don't worry.'

'Right! Agreed!' Strauss jumped in.

'Good. Don't go away.' Ray disappeared into the back of the store again.

I said to Strauss, 'If she's too abnormal for this place, can you imagine what she looks like? Do you want to travel with a severely handicapped girl? What if she's a monster?'

'Listen, the important thing is to get out of here. Then we can dump the girl at the first hospital or police station we come to. We'll tell them we found her wandering on the highway. They'll have to take care of her.'

'Right. Good thinking.'

We heard footsteps coming up from what had to be a cellar. *My God! The girl must be so abominable she has to be locked away!* I thought. I prepared myself for a shock. The curtain parted and Clem appeared. Behind him came a girl of about sixteen. There was only one word to describe her – *beautiful!* She had an angelic face, blond hair, blue eyes, and a lovely figure.

'This is my daughter, Clementine,' said Clem. We shook hands with the girl. She had a small suitcase with her. Just then we heard the sound of our car. I looked out the window and saw Herman parking it out front. I noticed it hadn't been washed, but I didn't care.

Strauss took Clementine's suitcase for her and led the way. I trailed behind. Clem detained me at the door and said, 'She's an ugly critter, ain't she?'

'I'm afraid so.'

'Been that way since birth.'

'Too bad.'

'You think some, whatchamacallit, plastic surgery would do her any good?'

'Oh, they're working wonders these days.'

'I'm sorry, I hope this isn't asking too much of you.'

'Oh, no, don't worry. We'll work it out just fine.'

We packed into the car, with Strauss driving and the girl between us. I was relieved to see that our belongings had been left untouched. Most important, we now had almost a half tank of gas. We gave Clem a friendly wave, made a U-turn, and headed back down the road by which we had come.

'Boy, what a relief to get out of that nut house,' said Clementine.

Strauss patted her bare knee, and I put my arm around her. 'For us too,' I said. Just touching her made my head swim. 'When we get home, you can settle in with me – uh, temporarily, of course.'

'And I'll get you a job,' said Strauss. 'You can work for me, in fact.'

In the light of the setting sun we spied yet another of Hezekiah's sayings on a billboard: *'Hezekiah Says: Green cheese is to black eye, as silvery moon is to starry-eyed, as honeymoon is to moon-eyed, as man in the moon is to private eye.'*

'My dear, I have a thousand questions to ask you,' said Strauss.

'I have one myself,' I said. 'What's the low-down on this guy Hezekiah? I mean, what's his game anyway?'

Clementine laughed. 'It's a long story, and you probably won't believe it.'

'Oh, yeah? Let's have it.'

And in the course of the next hour Clementine revealed the astounding, utterly shocking mystery of Hezekiah, a mystery – forgive me, dear reader – that the civilized world is not yet prepared to know.

Selected Potatoes

Ladies and gentlemen of the modern world, you who travel under the earth in tubes or ride complacently in great motor cars or sit within the comfort of your living rooms and watch television, you who trust that the sun shall set tonight and rise tomorrow, you who command complex machinery with the touch of a switch, you who write marks on papers and send them hither and yon in the name of Business, you who read newspapers and possess diplomas from accredited secondary schools and colleges, you who buy life insurance and subscribe to the *Reader's Digest* and other compendia of monotony, you for whom there is no Mystery left in Life: think now upon the Potato. Go to your kitchen cupboard or into your cellar and look closely at your bag of potatoes, or your box of instant mashed potatoes, or your bag of potato chips. Look for the words 'Selected Potatoes,' or perhaps 'Choice Potatoes,' and wonder to yourselves: How came these potatoes to be selected? By what miraculous human wisdom were these potatoes set apart from all others?

Behold, I explicate a Mystery kept secret since before your life began.

The sun shone bright on a Monday morning, as pretty a Monday morning as ever the industrious worker, clerk, agriculturist, or mere author of words might wish to see. In a three-storey warehouse such as those you pass every day without giving a thought to what might be transpiring therein, a momentous occasion was taking place – the birth of a new potato company, the Immortal Potato Company.

The President of this new enterprise, Major Theobald, a former cavalry officer, stood in the conference room at the head of the long table. Sitting before him were his Directors, all men of good breeding whom he had hand-picked, for Major Theobald was a Selector of Men, if not of potatoes. They eagerly awaited this inaugural and surely most historic address from their President.

'Gentlemen,' he began, 'today begins what we all hope shall be the magnificent and profitable life of the Immortal Potato Company. Shall we build it upon a foundation of clay, so that it might come tumbling down at any moment and cover its builders in the rubble of ignominy?'

'No! No!' they all replied as one.

'Or shall we build it upon a foundation of concrete and steel, that our edifice endure throughout the ages and shine forth like a beacon over the sea of human uncertainty?'

'Yes! Yes!' they replied with one voice.

'Oh, what a mistake it would be to follow the disastrous course of certain other potato companies, whose names shall not be mentioned within these walls, names that have become equated with all that is iniquitous, tawdry, and ephemeral in the domain of human enterprise. Breathes there a housewife who does not utter those names with bitterness, in the memory of sad experience with potatoes which have not been judiciously selected but have instead been offered in commerce as ... *mere potatoes?*' He shook his head sadly, eyes downcast for a moment. 'My friends, who among you relishes the prospect of going to his grave with the final conscious thought that he has had a hand in the vending of mere potatoes which have not been selected? Would any of you bequeath such a disgrace to your children and grandchildren? No, do not answer! I read the answer in your eyes.'

'My friends, as surely as Sin is punished, the world eventually but unfailingly metes out its cruel but righteous Judgment on those companies which do not select their potatoes but leave them on the doorstep, as it were, and run away like thieves in the night to count their petty and ill-gotten profits. And, therefore, I say to you, my Directors, my comrades, that before we do any one thing, before we dare look into the mirror and call ourselves Men of Business and Merchants of the Immortal Potato, we must first seek out and hire forthwith and without delay a Potato Selector, a professional person of knowledge and expertise, a man who would know both by instinct and by learned science how to select our potatoes. We would pay him any sum he might ask, even if it meant becoming debtors to one of the large banking establishments and remaining so for a very long period of time. Does any man among you disagree?'

'No! No!' cried one of the Directors, a man named Schultz, whom Major Theobald knew well from the cavalry – a man who had been wounded too many times to number in the valiant defense of a rural post office. 'We must indeed have a Potato Selector. But how are we to judge a candidate for such an important post? What would be his qualifications?'

'My very thoughts, noble Schultz,' said Major Theobald. 'Let us pause and think upon it for a moment.'

A silence fell over them as each man's hand (either right or left) moved pensively to his chin and slowly rubbed it or pulled upon the beard with a force calculated to stimulate the circulation of blood to the parts of the brain governing the highest abstractions of thought, as well as the most linear pragmatism. This period of silent cogitation lasted perhaps a minute or more.

Finally, Rudolph spoke up. 'He should be a tall man. Height makes a good impression. It inspires confidence and implies leadership and success.' There were mumblings of agreement.

Then Von Kleist spoke. 'But not too tall. For if he is too tall, he may hurt his back when bending over to inspect the potatoes. He should be sufficiently short so as to be close to them already. In fact, I would say he should have a tallness that carries a certain quality of shortness.' The other Directors applauded.

Then another of them, Walbrodt, spoke up. 'He should have maturity, for with maturity comes wisdom.'

'Yes, indeed,' said the Major, who was himself mature.

'But, of course, he will have to be rather young,' said Kepler, 'for we will certainly want him to live a very long time.' The group endorsed this view with words of affirmation.

'What else?' asked the Major. 'Farquahr, what is your opinion?'

The mild-mannered but nonetheless decisive Farquahr responded, 'He should be clean about his person. Well-groomed. His pants should be pressed and his shoes should be shined. He must present a good appearance to the public.'

'Is he to be seen by the public?' asked Gustavson.

'No. Nevertheless, a good appearance is essential for a man of his position.'

'Quite so,' the Major agreed. 'Anything else? Come, gentlemen, do not be shy. Much is at stake. Speak up.'

'Well,' said Dobrinsky, 'forgive me for mentioning it. It may not be relevant, but the thought had occurred to me ...'

'Yes, yes, out with it,' said the Major.

'Well ...' Dobrinsky looked around at his colleagues. 'The man should know his potatoes. How to pick them. How to know the good ones from the bad ones, as it were.'

'Hear! Hear!' they all said, slapping or banging the table in approval.

'I have a question,' said Humboldt, a retired Professor of Philosophy, whose position had been accidentally terminated by the complete destruction of his college at the hands of an arsonist and former pupil.

'Please share it with us, good Humboldt,' said the Major.

'Should he have his own potato selecting cane? Or are we to supply him with one?'

'Hmm,' said Major Theobald, suddenly plunged into doubt, as were all the others. 'We would not like to risk offending the man by such an oversight, would we?'

'No, no,' said the Directors.

'But, on the other hand,' he went on, tapping his index finger upon the scar on his chin he had received in a duel of swords at the age of nineteen. 'On the other hand, it would seem to me that if he were a true professional, he would already have his own potato selecting cane, custom-made perhaps for his own hand and height and length of arm and so forth. Does not the physician carry his own stethoscope? Does not the blacksmith work with his own anvil? Does not the sailor carry his own sextant?'

'A good sailor could use any sextant,' said Brébert, injecting a shrill note of contradiction, which caught the Major off guard and seemed to embarrass the others.

'Ahem, in any case, I am quite sure, for I have heard tell of it by acquaintances and read of it in the socially correct periodicals, that the Potato Selector prefers his own cane. And even if my memory deceives me in this respect, it stands to reason that if he is a true professional, he will already have one. Indeed, we might justifiably be suspicious of any candidate who presented himself for employment without his own cane. Why, he could be any sort of charlatan or scoundrel who might be clever enough to deceive us long enough to ruin our good names.'

'Yes, yes,' said the others, except for Brébert, who sat in a somewhat collapsed state, realizing his *faux pas* and now hoping to atone for it with an air of total submission and silence.

The Major looked at his Directors, each in turn, first clockwise, then counter-clockwise. 'I fear to ask it, but does anyone among you know of a Potato Selector whose services we might call upon and whom we could welcome to our bosom in a bond of everlasting trust?'

They shook their heads to say no, which did not surprise Major Theobald, as he was well aware not only of the extreme scarcity of practitioners of the art of potato selection but also of the probability, approaching zero, that a qualified candidate would at any given moment be unemployed and in search of a position.

'We could place an advertisement in the *Daily Enttäuschung*,' suggested Rudolph.

'Such would be expedient if our need were not so pressing, but in truth we require someone today – immediately, if not sooner,' replied Major Theobald. 'No, we cannot waste even one precious second. Gentlemen, I propose to telephone at once the Central Employment Bureau and ascertain whether they have within their vast files a qualified candidate.' This suggestion was greeted with comments of approval all around.

The Major picked up the telephone before him and asked the switchboard operator on the floor below to ring up the Central Employment Bureau. All eyes and ears waited with tense anticipation. The Major's eyes looked upward, as if in a silent prayer to the Lord.

'Hello? Kindly put me through to the Director himself, for no other personage can appreciate the gravity of my appeal. If he is in conference, I beg you to inform him of a call of the most urgent nature. If he is at tea, all the better, as the consumption of a finely brewed cup of tea, along with a dainty sweetmeat, will doubtless have effected a mood of good humor ... Hello? ... To whom am I speaking? ... Herr Wilhelm? It is Major Theobald, President of the Immortal Potato Comany, who importunes you on this fine morning ... Why, yes, the very same! ... Indeed, praise God! A fellow officer of the Second Dragoons! Oh, what a fine omen! ... Major Wilhelm, I call you upon a matter of great consequence, for this very day I have proclaimed and founded the Immortal Potato Company ... Thank you, kind sir! But a cloud of despair hangs above my head and the heads of my colleagues, who at this moment are sitting before me hoping and praying that you will be able to fulfill our most urgent need. We lack the one man without whom we would be but mere stumbling idiots destined for failure. We require a Potato Selector, for as you know, in the matter of potatoes ...' And here he stopped speaking and listened with the raptest attention to his interlocutor. Presently, tears of evident joy fell silently from the Major's eyes. He mumbled only 'yes, yes' at odd moments and nodded his head as he listened to the Director of the Central Employment Bureau. 'At once, Major Wilhelm! Send him at once! ... Yes, goodbye, and God bless you!' He hung up, his hand trembling.

'Tell us, Major Theobald! Pray do not leave us in suspense! What did he say?' asked Gustavson.

The Major took a kerchief from his breast pocket, the same breast that on national holidays could be observed bearing many medals won in the service of his country, and dabbed at his eyes. 'He said ... he said ... that at this very moment there sits outside his office, alone on a bench, a true and *bona fide* Potato Selector! And that this individual has sat there since Thursday, beneath the portrait of King Ludwig the Second of Bavaria, awaiting an offer of employment, and that his ceaseless repining has plunged the entire Central Employment Bureau into the deepest sorrow, for his pitiable sighs have echoed throughout the halls of that building to stab like hot knives into the tender hearts of its many clerks and officials, not the least of which the Director, the good and kind Major Wilhelm, a beloved brother officer of former days, numbers himself. But now, praise God, his sorrow and ours are at an end, and he comes to us, this very hour by the swiftest means available! I am assured that he is a man of integrity, perspicacity, and almost endless knowledge, an apprentice of the great master Zweig himself, and that he has returned after an absence of several years in the British Isles, where his skills have been sharpened to the greatest imaginable degree but where he finally succumbed to homesickness for his and our beloved native land! Truly, Providence has smiled upon us today, has it not?'

'Yes! Yes!' they exclaimed as one.

Then young Weinrich rose to his feet – unsteadily, for he was unused to addressing his elders. 'Oh, that men would praise the Lord for his goodness, for He has broken the gates of brass, and cut the bars of iron in sunder. He turns the fruitful land into a wilderness and back again, that the tillers of the fields might bring forth the potato. He pours His contempt upon the princes and causes them to wander where there is no way. We who sit in darkness, in the shadow of death, we hear the voice from above, and the stormy wind comes forth, the waves are raised up, the mountains are leveled to mere dust. As in the days of Moses, they murmured in their tents and hearkened not, and He overthrew their seeds among the nations, and so the plague was stayed. From His very girdle, wherewith He is girded continually ... We are tossed up and down as the locust … His great works … His … His … potatoes … Our souls rejoice … Our souls … I … Forgive me, I've lost my train of thought.' And so saying he sat down and covered his face with his hands and began to weep. His neighbors patted him on the shoulder.

'There, there, good fellow,' said Major Theobald. 'I'm sure we all comprehend your meaning, and even if not, we salute your eloquence all the same.'

Word soon spread throughout the building that the Potato Selector was coming. Each man and woman stood by his and her post – the baggers with their burlap bags, the labelers with their ink stencils, the clerks with their clipboards, the supervisors with their most officious countenances, the typists with their pretty, new ribbons, and even the lavatory attendant with his scrub brush. Did perhaps a thought of marriage or love flit like a fritillary in the mind of each unmarried girl? The ticking of the great clock in the lobby was but the external counterpart of each heart. A silence marred only by hushed whispers dominated the Immortal Potato Company. O foolish everyday world, that has no inkling of secret drama along the less traveled byroads of the City of Life!

At last there was a knock at the door. The Directors were all waiting to greet the Potato Selector. Major Theobald opened the door, and there stood the magnificent one himself – he who had been sent! He was a youngish man, yet with an air of maturity – modern-looking, yet at the same time possessing a certain classicism. One could tell that he was simultaneously of noble and common birth – that unique attribute that is found only among the great Potato Selectors. And it should be noted as well that he held a wondrous cane, whose well-worn handle bespoke a long and intimate association with him who held it.

'Good sir! We welcome you!' said Major Theobald.

The man stepped inside, removed his hat, and extended his hand. 'My name is Kovich. I am at your eternal service. From this moment on, my destiny is wedded to your own. Your call has come in answer to my silent prayers. My fleeting life, which, I must confess, appeared to have been cast into the abyss by the Fates and forgotten forever, is now lifted up again and bestowed with meaning.'

'Oh, good and kind sir! Noble sir! Noble Kovich! In your hands lie the fortunes of a hundred families – all whose homes and hearths are linked as if by invisible threads to our humble edifice! You have only to name your terms, be it rubies or pearls or the entire contents of our treasury!'

'Please, illustrious sir, do not speak of mundane materialism at this sublime moment of the heart! Do not think that I come to you compelled by thoughts of lucre, but rather by the fulfillment of my human mission. Oh, how my soul thirsts to select potatoes and thereby to disperse the dark clouds of anxiety from above your several brows and open the sky to the Light of Heaven! As for salary, the merest crust of bread, the merest pin money will suffice to sustain my earthly self. Now then, let us repair at once to the potato room, that I may being to make myself useful.'

And with these words, he followed Major Theobald to the third storey, with the Directors following the two of them and remarking among themselves: 'Note well his cane, how he handles it!' 'He walks like a saint!' 'What great secrets of potato-selecting science will he show to us?' 'The cut of his suit is quintessential beauty!' 'How his shoes shine!' 'How he parts his hair!' And so forth.

The solemn procession climbed up the stairs and walked onward toward the main potato room, and Kovich's feet trod upon the petals of rare flowers that had been purchased from a certain florist around the corner minutes before and were now strewn in his path by the ladies of the company.

The doors to the main storeroom lay open, and the staff stood in their places in rigid attention. Kovich paused just inside the threshold and beheld the great mounds of potatoes that had been carted in from the fields. He walked forward and picked up a potato, then turned and faced the Directors.

'If the potato be damned, it develops misshapenly, or else rots with fungus and invites the corruption of worms and centipedes. If the potato be blessed, it develops into a thing of beauty to gladden the heart of the housewife and nourish the bodies of her family. If it be neither blessed nor damned, it becomes the mere potato, which ought not be selected for the mouth of civilized man but allowed to return to the earth in the hope of greater grace for its future offspring. In this lies the challenge for the Man of Wisdom.' He examined the potato in his hand and looked into its eye. 'Verily, a Divine Spirit informs this potato.' And he gave it to the nearest bagger to be placed into her bag, which had been proudly stenciled to read *Selected Potatoes*.

82

And he lifted his cane and proceeded slowly among the potatoes, touching each one and declaring 'Yea' or 'Nay,' as the gatherers and baggers worked behind him.

The Directors wept openly in admiration as the great Kovich performed his miraculous work. And all the malignancies of the field and the terrible uncertainties of commerce and human existence were forgotten, and Beauty and Truth reigned throughout the land.

Did you not see the sun tinge the clouds with golden highlights? Did you not hear the songbirds chirping with joy? Did you not perceive the chorus of little angels above the Immortal Potato Company celebrating the miracle that was being worked *for you?* No, you brutish beasts, you earthen clods, you sticks of wood! You sat there stuffing your bellies with potatoes while poring over your silly newspapers, watching your insipid television programs, or prattling through spluttering lips your gossip and opinions, and about the banal and plebeian events of your vain and petty lives!

The Last Interview of Crad Kilodney

'Crad Kilodney? He's in the terminal ward,' said the head nurse to the pimply high school student in the red school jacket. The back of the jacket announced fiercely: GOLIATHS.

'I'm doing an essay for my English class.'

'Oh, you're the one. Now I remember. Just come this way, will you?' she said, with a mandatory terminal ward smile.

Two weeks before, the student had been told to write an essay on 'a famous and important contemporary writer, Crad Kilodney,' whom he had never heard of. He was failing the course and would need something special on this assignment. How fortunate, therefore, for him to have noticed the small article on page 40 of the *Toronto Sun* headed 'Lit Star Kilodney Close To Death' and to have recognized therein a wonderful opportunity to get some inside dope straight from the author.

The 40-year-old author was sitting up in bed smoking a cigarette and answering his fan mail, which came mostly from the United States. He was the only occupant in the bright three-bed ward. Golden light poured through the window. A single red rose in a pewter vase stood on the bedside table. Next to it lay a Pez candy dispenser, a tiny rubber kangaroo and a button that read 'Support Mental Health or I'll Kill You.'

The nurse left the student at the door. He stepped into the room. 'Hi, Mr. Kilodney?'

'Yeah.'

'I'm Phil Miasma. I called you about my essay for school. East York Collegiate, remember?'

'Have a seat.'

Phil picked up a chair and approached the bed, stopping suddenly. 'Are you contagious?'

'No, bring it up close. It's okay.'

He put down the chair, removed his jacket, draped it over the back and sat down, pen and pad at the ready. 'How are you feeling?'

'I'm dying.'

85

'I'm sorry.'

'It's okay.'

'What's wrong with you?'

'Brain abscess.'

'Does it hurt?'

'A bit.'

'How long until you, uh –'

'Croak.'

'Yeah, croak, ha ha.'

'Around nine o'clock tonight.'

'What! How do they know?'

'They have very exact methods.'

Phil looked at his watch. 'About six hours. Hey, you shouldn't smoke. It'll shorten your life span.'

'It's okay, they've already taken that into account.'

'Oh, okay. Well, um, I got these questions I thought up myself, like for my essay. I gotta hand it in tomorrow. I always put off essays till the last minute because I hate them so much.'

'Me, too.'

'I didn't know who you were when the teacher gave me the assignment. Everybody got somebody different. I only had time to read one of your stories because of basketball practice, but I bought the Coles notes. They explain everything.'

'Yes, they're pretty thorough.'

'But I thought, shit, I need something extra on this, like stuff from you personally to jazz it up, like, and nobody'd know where it came from. The teacher would really be impressed.'

'I get it. Okay, shoot.'

He clicked his pen. 'What do you use to write?'

'A pen.'

'What kind?'

'Ball point.'

'What do you write on?'

'Paper.'

'What kind?'

'White with blue lines on it.'

'Wow, this is far out!' Phil scribbled furiously. 'I know I'm gonna get an A. I wish I could get my paper all wrote up and marked by the teacher before you die so you could see what he says. He's a real jerk. His name's Mr. Voronoff.'

'Uh huh, I see.'

'How do you, like, get your shit together to write a story?'

86

'No problem. I just wait for inspiration.'

'How long does it usually take you to write a story, on the average?'

Kilodney stubbed out his cigarette and lit another. 'An hour.'

'Basically, like, what is the message in your writing?'

'What do you think?'

'I was going to write that it's that the whole world is just crazy, like, with people acting crazy all the time, right?'

'Uh, huh.'

'So, should I put that?'

'Sure.'

Kilodney reached for the buzzer to summon his nurse. 'What school did you say you're from?'

'East York Collegiate.'

'What does it say on the back of your jacket?'

'GOLIATHS.'

'Goliath was a Philistine, you know.'

'I heard he was a giant.'

'He was, but he was also a Philistine.'

'Hey, our basketball team's in first place, and I'm on it. I also play football.'

The nurse appeared at the door, smiling. 'Yes?'

'Morphine.'

She nodded and left.

Phil flipped a page. 'Who is you favorite author or the one who influenced you the most?'

'Henry Miller is my favorite.'

'What did he write?'

'*Tropic of Cancer*. Perhaps you've heard of it?'

'Oh, yeah, that dirty one, heh heh.'

'Not exactly.'

'What's your opinion of pornography? How far should a writer go?'

'I never thought about it.'

'You don't use too many dirty words in your writing, I notice.'

'No.'

'I read *Playboy* and *Penthouse*. My father's copies. They have some really good articles. You'd be surprised.'

The smiling nurse appeared with a syringe on a tray.

'Excuse me,' said Kilodney to his interviewer. Phil turned away and pretended to look out the window.

'You can turn around now,' said the author.

The student scanned his note pad for a moment. 'Ummm, what do you think is the importance of your work for Canadian literature?'

'I don't know.'

'What makes your work Canadian then?'

'I'm dying in Canada.'

'Right,' said Phil, writing the answer and underlining it. He turned back a page. 'Oh, I forgot this. I thought of writing this in my essay. Tell me if it's good. "He writes with a deep power in his words but obtains enough mildness when necessary." How's that?'

'Not bad.'

'I was thinking of being a writer myself some day. They give courses at York. I might go there. They have a good basketball team too.'

'Good idea.'

'Say, I was wondering. Could our English class come to your funeral? I'm sure it would be something they'd remember for the rest of their lives.'

'There isn't going to be any funeral. My body is going to the U. of T. Medical School for students to dissect.'

'Ugh! Disgusting! Of course, you'll be dead so you won't feel a thing.'

'Precisely.'

'Maybe they'll find out ...' Phil paused, eyes wide. 'Hey, I just thought of something!'

'What's that?'

'What if your crazy ideas all came from your brain abscess? What if your brain was sick right from the beginning?'

'It's entirely possible.'

'Then there was no talent involved. I mean, no offense. Like, shit, if you can be healthy and think up crazy ideas, that takes talent, but if they come automatically because of a diseased brain, it's like cheating almost. You see what I mean?'

'Uh huh.'

'Maybe I'd better not write that in my paper. I don't want to ruin your reputation.'

'Thanks. I appreciate that.'

'I hope nobody else thinks of it.'

'Me, too.'

Phil clicked his pen. 'That's it. I got no more questions. Thanks a lot. It was a great interview.'

'Don't mention it.'

He stood up and put on his jacket. 'Have you thought of what your last words will be?'

'No, not yet.'

'How about, umm ... Lemme think ... How about "Fuck you, world!" or "Get ready, God, here I come!" No wait, I got it! "Quick, bring me a lady Eskimo!" Gee, it's hard thinking up clever things to say.'

'I know.'

'If I get some ideas before nine o'clock, can I call you?'

'Sure. You can leave a message with the head nurse if I'm sleeping. She'll wake me up in time to die.'

'Okay, great.' He replaced the chair. 'It's been great meeting you. Sorry you gotta go. I'm sure the world will miss you.' He was already backing toward the door.

'Sure.'

'I promise to read all your books when basketball is over.'

'Thanks.'

'Well, see ya.' And he turned and left, the back of his school jacket flashing before the author's eyes for a split second. Kilodney smiled. Phil Miasma had provided him with a last word after all.

GOLIATHS.

Advanced Oboe Problems

1. The Enigma of Fatality

A death claim has reached the desk of Mr. Zwarun, age 26, of the Workers' Compensation Board. A worker in the research department of the Excelsior Oboe Company, Ltd., killed himself while testing a giant experimental oboe powered by an electric wind machine. Due to a miscalculation, the instrument emitted an infrasound wave of approximately 10 cycles per second at high amplitude. The worker fell dead instantly. His internal organs had been mashed into an amorphous jelly.

Mr. Zwarun must decide whether the company is liable for the worker's death, and, if so, to what extent. Did all the equipment used in the experiment belong to the company? Was the experiment done with the knowledge and approval of the company? Does the legal definition of 'oboe' extend to giant-size models?

Mr. Zwarun is wondering whether to open a new file for a new type of accident, which would require the approval of his superior. Now he is looking out the window of his sixteenth-floor office and suddenly realizes that what he has really wanted to do with his life is become a bass guitarist. Do you believe this would be a wise decision, career-wise?

2. The Uncertainty of the Poet

The poet laureate of Radford, Virginia, looked over her typewriter out her window and saw the cows coming down from the mountains. A little shepherd boy was leading them, playing an oboe, which he had made himself from primitive materials according to gypsy traditions. His gentle melody inspired the poet, who began to write:

> *Try to give an oboe*
> *That will be a lasting thing –*
> *That will, through tomorrow,*
> *Have a song to sing.*

She tore it up and began over:

Try to give an oboe
That memory and time will refine.
It may not seem much today,
But tomorrow the oboe will shine.

The poet left her typewriter and went into the bathroom.

Which of the following kinds of lines occur in the above text: amphibrach, choriambic, dactylic, anapestic, trochaic, iambic, detersive?

How would you compare the poet's style to that of Homer, Robert Lowell, or Edgar Guest?

How are we to interpret the poet's belief that the oboe will shine tomorrow?

3. The Conquest of the Philosopher

A philosoper answers the following ad in *True Men's Guts:*

'HEY GUYS! Tired of missing out on hot action? Now GET GIRLS by playing the oboe! Only $19.95 brings you easy instructions by the colored dot method plus song sheets of favorite oboe hits girls like!'

The philosopher buys a second-hand oboe and applies himself to the course diligently. Within two weeks he can play Schubert's *Die Forelle*. He then invites a freshman girl from his Logic 101 course home for dinner. Thereafter he seduces her.

Taking the seduction as the result, identify the efficient cause, formal cause, material cause, and final cause in the sequence of events. Are Aristotelian assumptions of causality 'true to life'?

4. The Nostalgia of the Infinite

Pinky Lee came into the kitchen, but he knew already there would be nothing to eat but ketchup and Ritz Crackers. His three children, all in their thirties, sat passively at the table with little bibs tucked under their chins. Mrs. Lee looked at him sadly and said, 'Pinky, there is no food, and we have no money left in the bank. If only you had saved more money from the show ... '

'Please, let's not go into that again.' Pinky put on his checked jacket and funny little hat and walked out into the evening air. Through the years Pinky had become closer to God and when pressed by doubts or exalted states of mind, he would try to get as close to God as possible. Since the completion of the World Trade Center, he had gotten very close indeed.

On his way up the elevator, Pinky thought of his birth in St. Paul, his early devotion to the oboe, and his success in the school band. Later when he contemplated a career in show business, he had an operation on his eyelids to modify his Chinese features so as to look Caucasian and not frighten children's television audiences of the mid-50's. He remembered all the times he sang, *Yo ho! It's me. My name is Pinky Lee!*, and how the smiling faces before him made it all worth while, despite the fact that the after-effects of the eyelid operation had turned him into a heroin addict, which cost him most of his earnings from the show.

Was Pinky dreaming, or was the speaker in the elevator emitting the poignant melody of Milhaud's *Oboe Concerto?* Wafted into the Infinite by his reverie, Pinky found himself sitting at the edge of the building, from which he could see the sun setting upon New Jersey. Or was it St. Paul? His body seemed filled with music, and he was at peace, and it was without a second thought that Pinky sang and danced his little dance right off the edge of the World Trade Center.

Will Pinky's family collect on his $ 100,000 life insurance policy? If a witness can be found to establish that Milhaud's *Oboe Concerto* was playing in the elevator and if medical evidence can be adduced to show its likely effect on Pinky's state of mind, can a case be made for accidental death? How would you argue the suit for the beneficiary? For the insurer? Is there a basis for *mens sana in corpore sano? Mens sibi conscia recti? Ars longa, vita brevis? Ex mero motu? Joci causa?* Does the oboe have a different effect on Chinese children than on Caucasian children?

5. The Mysterious Baths
A dead body is found wrapped in a sheet in a Turkish bath, with an oboe next to it. Explain.

6. The Archaeologists
Oboes have been found in Egyptian tombs dating back to the First Dynasty. Have your group act out a psychodrama called *The Archaeologists,* in which two archaeologists find the world's oldest oboe and must decide on its proprietorship. Roles to be assigned: two archaeologists (one male and one female), mummy, and high priest. Time limit: 15 minutes. Group discussion to follow.

7. The Enigma of a Day

The following is an extract from a book by a man who has devised a means of receiving messages from God by deducing code words or phrases from the events of the day:

Thursday, May 5th. 1970. Code phrase: *Requirements of a Vice President.*

Fixed rod in toilet to make it shut off. (Needs to be able to fix things out of adjustment.)

Woolworth – Got rubber stick-on soles for use on tennis shoes and other shoes. (Needs to be in good physical condition.)

Dentist – To get teeth cleaned. Assistant commented that I have a long upper lip from playing the oboe, which tends to stop one discolored tooth from showing. (Needs to have good personal appearance.)

Mail – A medical insurance ad. (Needs medical coverage.)

TV – Boy played the oboe in a youth talent show. (Needs to be talented.)

Life magazine with cover picture of Vice President. 'Spiro Agnew Knows Best,' 'Stern voice of the silent majority.' (Needs to be able to protect the interests of the majority.)

Puppy got head stuck in Marge's oboe. (Needs to be curious.)

Outside 7-11, blind man playing oboe asked for money. Gave him ten cents. (Needs to be charitable.)

Evaluate this extract from the viewpoints of: religion, psychiatry, general semantics.

Is the author's belief supernaturalistic, rationalistic or merely intuitive?

Do you agree with his choice of code phrase in this case?

8. Autumnal Melancholy

K. is poor and unknown and lives in a basement in a large North American city. He wishes to write something that will have sufficient impact on the world to change his life and lift him out of his misery. He has chosen the subject of oboes, but not for any particular reason. K. does not even play the oboe and had to look it up in a book to remember what it looked like. Assuming that K. is competent in the English language and has a great deal of time at his disposal, what should he write to accomplish his objective? Set up an equation expressing the probability of his success. Your equation should include factors relating to the social value of oboes, the number of persons likely to read K.'s work, and any assumptions you care to make about the forms of gratitude likely to be manifested by readers. Show all work and be neat. Send your solution to the author, who, in the meantime, is sitting patiently before a blank wall in a basement with a small window overhead, through which he can see red maple leaves falling from the trees.

ABOUT THE AUTHOR
Crad Kilodney is a one-man book operation, writing, editing,
publishing and selling most of his books on the street. He was born
in Queens, New York, and graduated from the University of
Michigan with a degree in astronomy. He has lived in Canada since
1973. His stories have appeared in over 70 magazines and
anthologies in the U.S., Canada and Great Britain, including the
prestigious 'Pushcart Prize' anthology. He is the founder of Charnel
House, his own imprint, and has also been published by Coach
House and Virgo Press. He has no formal training in
literature or creative writing.